PRAISE FOR
CURSE OF THE 1

A beautiful writing style draws young readers into this unique plot laced with valor, virtue, and humor. *Curse of the Komodo* is imagination and creativity residing comfortably with characters of reality. Readers will be waiting for the second book in this trilogy while forming fan clubs for their new favorite author.

Deanna K Klingel
Author of "Rebecca & Heart"

The power of transformation is a strong message, in the boys learning about love and compassion for their respective brother and for their grandfather. The animals use their traits to fight for each other, and for good to win over evil. As well, the curse is in fact a blessing, for in animal form they learn what matters most in life.

Kathleen Marusak

Joey, my 11-year old son, is a reptile enthusiast! As we were reading *Curse of the Komodo* together, we made so many text-to-world connections between the story, his knowledge of reptiles, and our frequent visits to the Detroit Zoo and the Toledo Zoo. We can't wait for *90% Human!*

Randy and Joey Maddock
Troy, Michigan

Curse of the Komodo is a fun read for young adult readers as well as adults! Filled with animal facts and a spell-binding story, this book hooks readers from start to finish!

L. Burnham
Teacher, Toledo, Ohio

90%
Human

90% Human

M.C. Berkhousen

Illustrations by Kalpart

Progressive
RISING PHOENIX PRESS ®

Published 2018 by Progressive Rising Phoenix Press, LLC
www.progressiverisingphoenix.com

ISBN: 978-1-946329-75-2

Printed in the U.S.A.
1st Printing

Edited by Carol Gaskin

Book Cover Design by Kalpart
Visit www.kalpart.com

Front Cover illustration by Kalpart

Book design by William Speir
Visit: http://www.williamspeir.com

For Alyssa and Mariden

Acknowledgements

It takes a lot of people to get a book from the author to the reading public. First, my thanks go to Amanda Thrasher and the production team at Progressive Rising Phoenix Press for their help in publishing this book. A special thanks to the artist at Kalpart for the cover design and art work, and to the folks at Ingram/LSI for producing a beautiful book.

Thanks also to my supportive and helpful editor, Carol Gaskin, for polishing the manuscript and making it the best it could be. Thank you Tim Herman, herpetologist, for answering questions about animals, and to Connor and Evan Muse for helping me with plot points.

A special team of people read the manuscript to find any mistakes or content issues. Thank you Leslie Burnham, Pamela Kelso and Jennifer Muse for your thoughtful review, helpful comments about events at the camp and ongoing encouragement. Thanks also to readers Riley Park, Sara Roza, Tim Wiemer, Maxwell Kelso, and David Wiemer for reading the manuscript and providing helpful feedback about specifics. First Draft Writers, my writing critique group, provided feedback and suggestions throughout the development of this book. Thank you Pamela Kelso, Judith Scharren, Joette Rozanski and Charles Abood.

Last, I'd like to thank the most important group, my readers! You are the reason I write.

M.C.

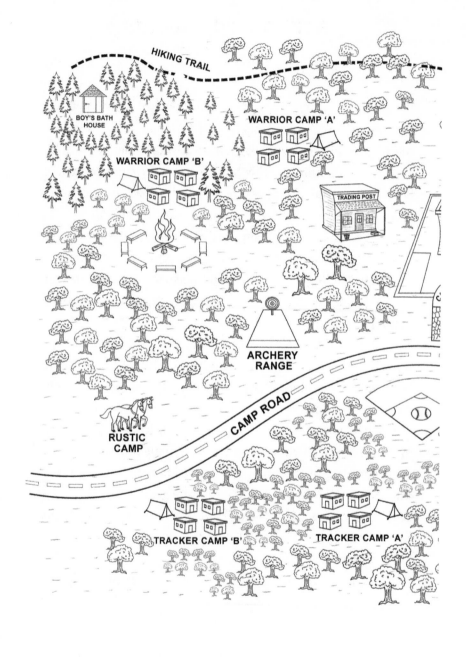

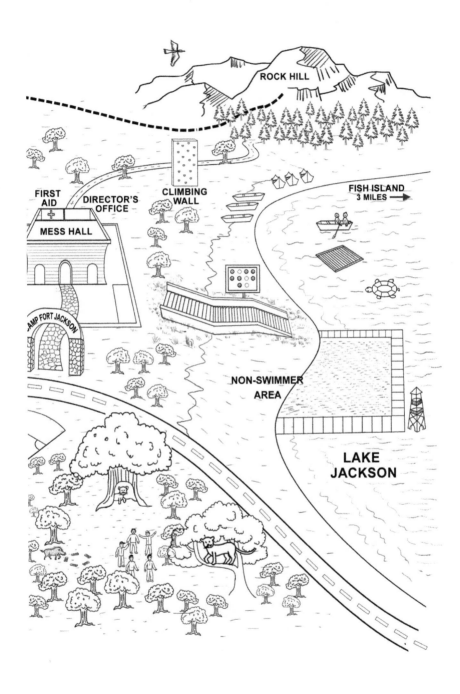

ROCK HILL

FIRST AID

DIRECTOR'S OFFICE

CLIMBING WALL

FISH ISLAND
3 MILES →

MESS HALL

CAMP FORT JACKSON

NON-SWIMMER AREA

LAKE JACKSON

Table of Contents

Chapter One—Camp Fort Jackson

Marshmallow and chocolate oozed down my hand from between the graham crackers. I took a bite and licked my sticky fingers. Yum. S'mores were the best thing about campfires. My brother sat on a log across from me, eating around the sides of his S'more. His third. Not that I was keeping score.

We'd both been sent to Camp Fort Jackson in Michigan for two weeks. I liked camp, but Austin didn't. He was more of a "hotel" camper. He liked heated indoor pools, movies on the TV, and calling for room service. He especially liked hotels where housekeeping turned down the beds and left little wrapped chocolates on his pillow.

Going to camp was my favorite vacation. Listening to the wind rustling trees around me, I felt quiet inside. When darkness settled over the forest, I could hear the creep and howl of nocturnal animals. Some nights the counselors let us bring our sleeping bags outside and sleep on the ground around the campfire. As we lay on our backs and gazed up, the sky seemed like a big bowl of twinkling stars, tipped over to form a dome around us. We'd often see shooting stars. Comets.

Those were the times I wished Gramps was at camp with us so he could tell us about them.

My group was the Warriors, the unit of the camp for older kids with more camping experience. Austin's unit, the Trackers, was for kids ten to twelve years old. Both groups were divided into two sections, Section A, for girls, and Section B, for boys. Tonight the Warriors and the Trackers—boys' sections—had gotten together for a hotdog roast. Before we cooked the hotdogs, the Warriors showed the Trackers how to build a campfire. Austin already knew, because I'd shown him that a long time ago.

Mom told Austin he didn't have to go to camp, but he insisted on signing up. I had the feeling he was here to keep an eye on me. I wasn't sure why. He didn't know about my secret. No one knew. Not even Mom or Dad. I'd been very careful to keep it to myself. I always wore tee shirts so no one could see the downy feathers under my arms. If anyone found out, they'd probably send me to a hospital and dissect my body for research.

Terry, one of our counselors, threw a couple of logs onto the fire, sending sparks up into the air. The flames leapt higher, throwing orange light across my brother's face. He was wiping marshmallow from his fingers with one of those little packaged wet wipes.

Then Terry started a song. It was one of those songs you only sing at camp, and nowhere else. Since this was my fourth year at camp, I knew all the words. It was Austin's second year at camp and he knew all the words too. Any factoids that crossed Austin's path were quickly devoured by his brain. He remembered everything he read and everything he heard. He could list everything he got for Christmas five years ago. He probably even remembered his birth.

Our other counselor, Levi, handed around packets of mosquito repellent. I tore the package open and rubbed the mosquito repellant wipe over my face and neck. It smelled like butter that had been left out in the sun for three days. I didn't care about the smell as long as it worked. Camp mosquitos left bites the size of a quarter.

Austin pushed himself up from his log and came around to my side of the fire. He sat down next to me. "What do we have to do to get out of this place early?" he whispered.

I slapped a mosquito off my neck. "Why? Don't you like it?"

"Tonight was okay, but the food in the mess hall sucks."

I laughed. "I thought you weren't going to complain about food anymore."

Austin sighed. "Okay. I take it back. The food here is a lot better than the food at the zoo."

He wasn't talking about the burgers, fries, and hotdogs they sold at the zoo's restaurant or food carts. He was talking about food that was fed to the bears and reptiles. Austin and I had spent three days at the zoo last fall, but not as visitors.

We'd gone to the zoo on a school field trip. A really wild storm came up, and lightning hit the water tower. The next thing we knew, Austin and I were on the wrong side of the animal exhibits. I'd become a scaly, dangerous Komodo dragon. Austin, who quit karate class because he was afraid of hurting someone, had turned into the world's tamest grizzly bear. We were trapped inside those animal bodies for three days. The zookeepers fed us the things zoo animals eat. Frozen rats. Raw fish. Warmed-up dead rabbits.

Our grandfather, who teaches physics and astronomy at the college in town, came to find us. He rescued us and helped us change back into humans. Our lives had been pretty normal since then, except for one thing. When we got home from the zoo, I found tiny white feathers under my arms. They were left from when I turned into an eagle to rescue a friend. I only had feathers on less than ten percent of my body, so I figured I was still ninety percent human. After what Austin and I had been through, that was good enough. I was grateful just to be home.

Now school was out and we were at summer camp. I was in a cabin with five other guys. One was Jim Cox, who was also my "buddy" for swimming and hiking. The other four were Jerry Hill, Matt Philips, Jake Parma, and Bill Carlson. Jerry and Matt were swimming buddies; so were Jake and Bill. Buddies had to stick together, especially during water sports, riding, or hiking in the woods. Buddies kept an eye on each other. It was a safety thing.

Jake came around the fire to sit next to me. I moved away from him, but I wasn't fast enough. He'd already grabbed the skin above my waist and was pinching as hard as he could. I yelped in pain.

"What's the matter?" asked Austin. He was on my other side and couldn't see what Jake was doing. "Did you get stung or something?"

"What's the matter, little baby?" Jake used a high, squeaky voice. He pinched me again, twisting my skin beneath his fingernails. It was so painful I almost got tears in my eyes. I jumped up, rubbing my side. I wanted to punch Jake in the mouth, but the camp had zero tolerance for fighting. We could both be sent home.

"Mommy's little baby has delicate skin," chirped Jake. "Little baby Lukey makes me want to pukey."

"Knock it off, Parma." Levi walked over to our side of the fire. "Go to the cabin and get on your bunk. Stay there until I say you can get off."

"What about him?" Jake pointed at me. "He started it."

"He didn't do anything to you," said Jim. "Looked to me like you were doing something to him."

"Did Jake do something to you?" Levi's voice was low and kind, but the guys still heard him. Everyone was staring at me. Bill, Jake's buddy, grinned.

"Nope," I said. "A mosquito bit me."

Jake's pinches hurt bad, but there was no way I'd tell a counselor. The camp didn't tolerate bullying, so the counselor would report it to the camp director, Mrs. Harris. She would tell the camp nurse. The nurse would examine me and find the feathers. I'd never be able to explain how I got them. No one would believe what really happened.

Levi was still waiting. "Answer me, Luke. Did Jake do something to you?"

I shook my head again. "Nope."

"You sure?" asked Levi. "Why are you rubbing your side?"

"Mosquito bite."

Levi lowered his voice. "We'll talk about this later."

The other counselor, Terry Miller, started another song, and Levi passed out more graham crackers, chocolate squares, and marshmallows. I gave mine to Austin. My side hurt so much I couldn't eat. I wished I could turn back into a Komodo just long enough to gobble up Jake Parma. I wouldn't have to totally swallow him. Just one little bite would do it. That's all it would take to inject enough Komodo venom to cause him a lot of pain and send him to the hospital.

Why was Jake doing this? I'd never met him before camp, but he seemed to be out to get me for some reason. I usually really liked camp, but Jake was ruining it. I watched him walk to our cabin, kicking leaves and twigs out of his way. I didn't like him being in there alone. He could go through my suitcase, eat the candy bars I had hidden, wreck or even steal my stuff.

I got up to walk to the restroom. Austin shoved himself up from his log and followed me. I told Levi where we were going and that we'd be right back. The bathhouse, which contained showers and toilet stalls, was about a hundred yards away on the other side of a small pine forest. The trees made it smell like Christmas. The woods were dark and filled with shadows, so we aimed our flashlights at the ground to light the path.

"You didn't have to come with me," I said.

Austin's voice came from behind me. "I had to go. Besides, I don't trust that Parma kid. Can't you get moved to another cabin?"

"I'd have to explain why."

"So explain. He deserves to get into trouble."

Jake would only get into trouble, but I'd be exposed as a freak! I didn't know what to say, so I didn't answer.

In the bathhouse, I went to the sink and washed my hands. I didn't have to go to the bathroom. I just wanted to get away from the other kids for a little while.

"When's that roping clinic you're going to?" asked Austin.

"Tomorrow." I ran cold water on a paper towel and held it on my side. Austin watched me, frowning.

"Maybe you could get transferred to horse camp."

I shook my head. "I'm afraid I'd make the horses nervous. I think they'd sense the Komodo. Even though I don't show it, it's never very far away."

Austin nodded. "I feel that way about the grizzly too. If I got angry, it might come out when I don't want it to." He was quiet for a few seconds, staring at the concrete floor. A daddy longlegs spider was walking toward the drain. Austin moved his foot away so he wouldn't step on it. Then he said, "Let's say you get good at roping. How will you use it? There aren't many jobs for cowboys anymore."

I ran cold water on the paper again. When I looked up, Austin's eyes met mine in the mirror. He licked his lips. "You think we're going to the island, don't you."

He was so freakin' smart. I sighed. "It's a possibility. If any of our animal traits get worse, we might not have a choice."

Neither of us said the name "Komodo Island." A mysterious place, far, far away, occupied by a gigantic reptile that had humans on its list of prey. A reptile that could run faster than most humans, swim, and eat a goat in two bites.

"You're going to need help," said Austin. "Say we corner a big one and it's pink. It's bucking, snorting, and trying to eat everybody in sight. And that's after we shoot it with the tranquilizer gun."

"Maybe it won't come to that." I took the paper towel off my side and examined the skin. There was a big purple spot with four fingernail dents in the center.

Austin lifted my shirt. "What's going on with your back, Luke? You're covered with bruises. Did Jake do this to you?" He frowned with anger. "You can't let him get away with this. You have to do something about it."

"I wish I had some ice." I put another cold paper towel against my side and leaned back against the counter.

"I'll get you some ice. There's an ice machine near the mess hall." Austin crossed his arms and leaned against the counter next to me. "We could fix Parma good, you know. He deserves it."

I shook my head. I just couldn't risk it. Besides, I'd dealt with a much worse bully than Jake. "Do you remember how that night guard, Dunn Nikowski, zapped us with that cattle prod when we were in the bodies of zoo animals?"

"It burned like fire," said Austin. "Jake reminds me of him for some reason."

"He's a bully, that's why."

"There's one big difference between them," said Austin. "Jake is alive and well. Dunn Nikowski is dead." Austin shoved himself away from the sink. "How can you sleep with that guy in your cabin? Maybe I should hang out next to your cabin and watch through the window." Then he grinned. "One good shake from a grizzly would teach him a lesson."

"Or just a little Komodo venom," I added.

Laughing, we went back to the campfire. Austin sat down in my place, next to Jake, who'd been allowed to come back to the campfire. Jake looked down at him and sneered.

"I don't sit next to Trackers." He got up and went to the other side of the campfire, giving us the finger behind his back. For the rest of the evening, he sat staring at the dirt. He was probably thinking up more ways to make trouble.

How could I stop Jake from bullying me? A fight would result in both of us being sent to the director, and then to the nurse. I had to avoid that, no matter what. I couldn't let anyone see those feathers. There had to be another way to teach Jake a lesson.

The next morning I woke up so early it was still dark. I grabbed my shower bag and walked down the wooded lane to the bathhouse. I turned on my flashlight so I could see where I was going. Squirrels scampered across the path in front of me. Birds shrieked and flew away, as if they were angry I'd awakened them. The bathhouse was completely dark inside. Running my hand across the cold concrete wall, I found the light switch. I flipped it on. Something brown with yellow stripes was coiled in a corner. A garter snake stretched out to a length of about four feet and oozed across the floor. It disappeared through a hole under the door.

Standing in front of the mirror, I raised my arms and studied the feathers. I wished I could get rid of them. Swimming in tee-shirts was boring. I was sick of worrying about them all the time. More than anything, I wanted to be like the other guys. If I didn't have these stupid feathers I wouldn't have to wear a tee-shirt to swim.

I grabbed a feather and yanked it out. It hurt, a lot. Could I shave them off? Probably not. The shaft of the feather, the thing that connected it to my skin, was too thick for a razor. Grabbing another feather, I yanked again. It felt like I'd been stung by a wasp. I'd never get rid of the feathers out that way. There were too many of them and it hurt too much.

Then I remembered something. When Gramps was young, he lived on a farm. If his mother wanted to make a chicken dinner, she'd catch one of the chickens and chop off its head. Gramps said the chicken's body would run around for a few seconds without its head. Then his mother would grab the chicken by the feet and dip it into a pail of very hot water. The hot water loosened up the feathers so they were easier to pluck. According to Gramps, it only took a few minutes to get all the feathers off.

I ran my hand across the rows of downy feathers under my arms. No way was I going to dunk myself in hot water. Maybe a hot shower would help.

I showered, lathering myself up with soap and hot water. When I was finished, I dried off and went back to the mirror. I tugged on a feather. Nothing happened. To get it out I had to yank really hard, just as before. The feather finally came lose, but it stung as badly as it had before my shower. I gave up and finished dressing. Before I left the bathhouse, I picked up the three feathers I'd pulled out and rolled them into my towel. By the time I got back to the cabin, the other guys were just getting up.

While they were showering, I hung my towel on the clothesline. The feathers fell to the ground. Jim, my "buddy," was just getting back from the bathhouse. His eyes widened when he saw the feathers on the ground.

"These are eagle feathers, Luke!" He picked them up and rubbed them gently between his fingers. "They're from a bald eagle. Where did you get them?"

"I found them near the bathhouse." It was almost the truth. There was no point in trying to lie about it. Jim was Native American. He'd recognize eagle feathers right away.

"They're protected by law," said Jim. "You'll have to turn them over to the Fish and Wildlife Service."

"I thought Native Americans could have them for religious services."

"We can, but we have to apply to the Fish and Wildlife department to get them." He handed me the feathers. "You'd better give these to a counselor. You can get big fines for keeping them. You can even go to jail."

Great. Now I had another worry. If I did yank the feathers out and was caught with them, I could go to jail. I hoped I wouldn't start molting.

Jim and I walked together to the dining hall. Breakfast was hot cereal with raisins, walnuts, and brown sugar or cold cereal with bananas. While I was filling my bowl with corn flakes, I spotted Austin. He didn't look happy. He was staring at the bowl of oatmeal in front of him. Austin didn't like oatmeal. He preferred omelets with onions, peppers, and cheese for breakfast, with toast and jam and a cup of Court Lodge—a fancy decaf tea. Instead, he was getting mushy porridge and orange juice from a can.

I felt bad for him. He didn't want to be here. The only activity Austin liked at camp was the climbing tower. He could climb that thing upside down and backwards, like Batman. I didn't do the climbing tower because I was afraid of heights. I waved and Austin waved back, his mouth twisted in a half-smile. Several Tracker girls came to sit with him. His face lit up, and the half-smile turned into a first-class grin.

Campers had to help with getting meals on and off the table. After breakfast, the assigned campers cleared the tables and returned food and dishes to the counter between the kitchen and the dining room. That morning, it was my job. I was heading toward the kitchen with a pile of plates when I heard a familiar female voice.

"Stop it, Jake!" It was Megan Gifford. Jake Parma was reaching for the necklace she was wearing. The guy was just obnoxious.

"I just want to see it," said Jake. "Is that a lizard on that shell? Just let me look at it for a minute." He stretched out his hand again, and Megan batted it away.

"I said no! You'll take it and hide it somewhere, and I'll never get it back." She picked up some cereal boxes and brought them to the counter.

"Hi, Luke."

I set my stack of plates on the counter and turned around. Megan grinned at me. She'd grown a little. She was still about four inches shorter than me, but she looked different. Older. Prettier, maybe.

"I didn't know you were here," I said. "Which group are you in?"

"Trackers," said Megan. "Section A. I turn thirteen next month, so I really should be in Warriors." She put down the cereal boxes and took a lunch sack and a water bottle from the counter.

"Going on a hike?" I asked.

"Yes. We're going around the lake to see if we can spot some animals. We can either sketch them or take pictures. I'm taking a camera."

She was wearing a necklace made of beads. From it hung a shell, painted with the image of a pink Komodo. I tried not to stare at it, but the shell seemed to be glowing a little, like a dim flashlight.

"Megan, is that shell changing color?"

She took it off and gaped at it. "It's lighting up, like it has a pink bulb inside. I've never seen it do that before."

I couldn't help staring at that necklace. I knew where it came from, although I didn't think Megan did. It was very old and was connected to the mysterious curse that caused us to become zoo animals the previous fall. Gramps told us about the curse and how it happened. He and a friend, Dunn Nikowski, were on Komodo Island, on leave from the U.S. Navy. Dunn poked a Komodo with a stick. It attacked him and bit his leg. Gramps shot the Komodo, then got Dunn to the island's hospital. Dunn lost his leg and was very ill. A medicine woman came to Dunn's room and put a necklace made of beads around his neck. Now, fifty years later, Megan Gifford was wearing that same necklace. Before I could ask to see it, another girl called to Megan from across the room.

"Come on, Megan," she said. "You can talk to your boyfriend later."

Megan's face flushed from her chin all the way to her forehead.

"I'm ...so sorry," she stuttered. "I didn't say you were my boyfriend. I said I wanted to say hi to a friend, that's all."

"No worries." I kept my tone casual, pretending girls said that stuff about me all the time.

Megan was already tearing across the dining room. "Thanks for embarrassing me, Louise," she said as she flew out the door.

Jim was waiting for me by the counter. He sucked in his cheeks, trying not to laugh.

"She's not my girlfriend," I muttered. "She's just a nice kid who's in Austin's class at school. She's only twelve or thirteen years old."

The truth was, Megan was more that "just a nice kid." She had saved my life, and I'd saved hers. We were friends. I didn't know how to explain all that to Jim. He was still grinning at me.

"Like I said, she's just a kid. A lot younger than me," I explained.

"She looked older," said Jim. "And you'd look good together. Pretty red hair—just like yours. Pretty face, pretty..." He started making a woman's shape in the air with his hands. I glared at him. He held up his hands in surrender.

"Let's get back," I grumbled. "We have inspection in ten minutes."

Levi and Terry inspected our cabin every morning. Jim and I had made our beds and tidied our area before we left for breakfast, so there wasn't much left to do. We just had to make sure our suitcases and storage areas were neat.

When we arrived at our cabin, the other guys were already inside. Their bunks were made, and their suitcases were open and neatly arranged. But one side of the cabin was a mess. The blankets from the upper and lower bunks were tangled and hanging half on the floor. Two suitcases lay open and all the clothes were bundled up on the mattresses.

"What happened to my bunk?" I yelled.

"We had this stuff ready for inspection before we went to eat," cried Jim. "Who did this?"

"I don't know," said Bill. "It was like that when we got back from breakfast. I was kind of surprised. You guys are usually pretty neat."

I glanced at Jake. He was lying on his bed, reading a book. The book was upside down. He was smiling. I was so angry I started to tremble. I could feel the prick of scales just under my skin. My mouth began to water and the muscles in the back of my throat clenched, ready to swallow something.

My whole body was ready to turn Komodo. Everything in me ached to get back at Jake. All it would take was one little bite. They'd have to take him away in an ambulance, and that would be the end of Jake's camping days for this year.

I took a deep breath and shook the thought away. I couldn't let myself use my animal traits that way, no matter how angry I was. Taking another deep breath, I closed my eyes. Slowly, my body started to feel normal again. My hands stopped shaking.

I picked up some shirts from the floor. They were wet and slimy, covered with something white. Toothpaste!

Levi and Terry knocked on the door, then stepped inside. They scanned the cabin, nodding approvingly at the orderly bunks and suitcases. Levi stared at the two rumpled bunks with the clothes dumped on top of them.

"Whose bunks are these?" asked Terry.

"Mine," I said through clenched teeth. I pointed to the lower bunk next to me.

Jim shoved some stuff aside and patted his upper bunk. "This one is mine." He let out a long, discouraged sigh.

"You two will miss swimming this morning while you clean up your areas," said Terry.

Levi cleared his throat. "Jake, what's that you're reading?

"*Divergent,*" said Jake.

Levi took the book from his hand, turned it right side up and handed it back to him. Everything got very quiet. Jim stood still, his arms full of clothes. My heart started to pound. It took all my self-control not to grab Jake and fling him out the door.

Levi looked at me steadily for a few seconds. "Do you have anything to say about this, Luke?"

Thoughts swarmed in my head. If I told on Jake, we'd go right to the camp director's office. Levi would report everything he'd seen. He'd tell the director he'd seen Jake pinch me. The director would send me to the nurse. Miss Powell would look at my arms and maybe my back. She'd see the bruises. Then she'd see the feathers, and within an hour I'd be in an ambulance heading for the nearest large hospital that had a research laboratory. I couldn't let that happen.

Levi was still waiting. I shook my head. Levi glanced at Jim. "You have anything you want to say about this?"

"No," said Jim. He crossed his arms and stared at the floor.

I shot him a grateful look. I wasn't sure why Jim didn't report Jake, but I was glad he had my back.

With one more glance at Jake, Levi followed Terry outside. I looked out the window and watched them walk across the clearing to the next cabin.

Grinning, Jake pushed himself up from his bunk. "Too bad you have to miss swimming, pukey Lukey. You shouldn't be so messy." He grabbed the back of my arm and pinched it.

That did it. Flattening my hand, I chopped the inside of Jake's elbow as hard as I could. His arm flopped limply to his side. His face turned red as he scrunched up his mouth.

"You'll pay for that, Pukey." His voice was hoarse. "You better watch your back."

I moved closer to him and stared up into his face. "Ooooohh. I'm really scared. Touch me again and you'll be crawling out of here."

Jake backed away from me. His eyes never left me as he grabbed his towel. Hurrying out, he slammed the door. The other guys followed him, grim expressions on their faces.

Jim and I remade our beds and put our suitcases and storage bins back in order. Jake had squirted toothpaste over my clothes, so I had to spend two hours washing them by hand.

Levi came into the bathhouse while I was still scrubbing toothpaste out of my jeans. It wasn't coming out very well. White streaks still showed on the dark cloth.

"Not being a snitch is one thing," said Levi. "But letting that kid bully you is unacceptable. Why won't you be honest about what he's doing to you?"

"I can't prove he messed up my stuff. I didn't see him do it. Besides, I think I've got it handled."

Levi's expression was stern. "This camp has zero tolerance for bullying. Next time I'll report it whether you do or not. Got it?"

I nodded and went back to work on my jeans. Levi shook his head and walked away. I hated that he was angry with me. It was like he was blaming me for this, and it wasn't my fault. Levi didn't know my secret. If I told on Jake, I would be the one who would suffer the most. It wasn't fair. I hated the situation I was in. I hadn't asked for these stupid feathers. They were caused by something I did when we were trying to get Megan out of the zoo.

We'd gone back to the zoo to rescue her. She was still in the form of a death adder when Dunn hid her on top of the zoo's water tower. Somehow she fell off. When I saw the small red snake falling through the air, I instantly turned eagle to catch her. It wasn't even a decision. But it was my fourth change, and according to the curse, the fourth time you changed form, you stayed that way. I did go back to my human form, except for one little thing. I still had tiny white feathers under my arms.

It took all morning to remake our beds, scrub the toothpaste out of our clothes, and hang them on the clothesline to dry. Jim and I finished just in time for lunch. We ate hamburgers and fries, with ice cream for dessert. I glanced at my watch. I had just enough time to get to the roping clinic. I was going to be needing primo lassoing skills in the future.

Chapter Two—Roping Clinic

The roping clinic was being held at Rustic Camp, the part of Camp Fort Jackson where they taught riding and the care of horses. It was called "Rustic Camp" because the campers lived in primitive cabins and ate all their meals outdoors. There were no nice bathhouses with showers, either. Campers used metal Porta Potties and swam in the lake or washed in a primitive shower facility to get clean.

The campers cared for the horses, including "mucking out" their stalls. "Mucking out" meant shoveling up the manure and dirty straw, sweeping the floor, and then putting down clean straw. Campers also fed, bathed, and groomed the horses. It was a lot of work. But it was fun too. I'd gone there for the past two years and learned to be a pretty good rider.

Austin and I walked the half mile to the entrance of Rustic Camp. We made a right turn, passed some cabins, and followed the driveway to the corral, where a group of kids had gathered.

Two horses were drinking water from a trough next to the fence. When Austin and I walked past the corral, both horses backed away. They snorted and sniffed; then one horse reared. The other horse whinnied, pawing the ground. Then it turned and ran away.

The instructor, a woman who looked about the same age as our mom, watched them go. She glanced at us, looking confused.

"We didn't do anything," I said, holding out my hands. "We didn't even go near the corral."

I knew why the horses had shied away from us. They could sense the animal traits that were still left over from our time at the zoo. A Komodo dragon would send them running for sure. So would a bear. The horses must have been very confused when they saw us. Outwardly we were just kids, like the other campers. But somehow they could sense that a dangerous reptile and a grizzly bear were just a few breaths away.

"That's so odd," said Mrs. Callahan. The horses were now in the farthest end of the corral, huddled together near the fence. "Maybe a bee stung one of them." She glanced at her watch. "Let's get started."

First she gave us each a rope. These ropes were heavier and a little stiffer than ordinary ropes. Holding the tip or end of the rope, Mrs. Callahan showed us how to make a slip knot, or "honda." We fed the rope through the honda to make a loop. The goal was to get this loop over a steer's horns.

Our "steer" was a bale of hay with a plastic steer head on one end. The head had very long horns. Those horns were our target. Our job was to learn to swing the rope, aim the loop, and lay it over the dummy steer's horns.

Most of the class members were campers who wanted to learn roping so they could be in rodeo competitions and rope calves. They would have to do everything we were learning while riding a horse. Austin and I wouldn't be on horses or in roping competitions. We wanted to be able to rope something stronger and much more dangerous than a calf. Our target would be bucking, hissing and trying to eat us as we tried to lay the loop around its scaly neck and legs.

During the clinic we practiced swinging the loop and letting it fly, hopefully landing over the dummy steer's horns. On the third try I managed to throw the loop around one horn. Mrs. Callahan showed me how to position my hand so the loop would catch both horns. It wasn't easy, but by the end of the class I had done it twice. For once I caught on faster than Austin. Maybe it was because I'd watched the kids roping the year before, when I went to horse camp, so I'd already gone over it many times in my mind.

The clinic lasted for almost two hours. We stopped for a break after an hour and sat under nearby trees to drink water and eat potato chips. By the end of the second hour, Austin and I were tired and ready to go back to our own camp. There would be another clinic on Saturday.

We thanked Mrs. Callahan and said goodbye to the other campers. Then we trudged back up the hill to our own camp.

Warriors second swim period was later that afternoon. I couldn't wait. Jim and I had missed the morning swim because we failed inspection, so we were both eager to get into the water. I changed into my swimsuit, keeping my tee shirt on to cover the feathers. Jim and I walked down to the lake together. The lake was at the bottom of a steep hill. To get there, campers had to walk down one hundred and five wooden steps. At the bottom of the steps was a big wooden board with round tags that hung on wooden pegs. Each of us had a tag with our name on it. One side of the tag was red, and the other side was white. Before going into the water, we turned the tag to the red side. After we came out, we turned it back to white. That way the lifeguards knew everyone was out of the lake.

We also had to swim close to our buddies. When the lifeguard blew the whistle, we had to join hands and hold them up while they counted heads. The camp had other safety rules for swimming and watercraft skills as well. If you didn't obey the rules, you could lose your lake privileges.

About one hundred yards from the shore, a big square raft rocked lazily against the ripples. Before we could swim out to it, we had to pass a swimming test. Jim and I were both good swimmers. We had passed the test the first day, so we could swim to the raft anytime we wanted. I liked to get out there first and stretch out on the raft. It was fun to feel it rock back and forth when the motorboats went by. Sometimes we saw big fish swimming beneath the raft. Unfortunately, Jake and Bill passed the swim test too. I saw their heads bobbing in the water as they swam toward the raft. That was the end of our peace and quiet.

"You wearing that shirt again today, Brockway?" Jake pulled himself up onto the raft. "We haven't seen the sun in two days."

"Clouds don't protect you from sunburn." I turned my head away.

He shook his head. "What a wimp. Come on, guys. Who wants to swim across the lake?" He dove off the far side of the raft and started out.

The lifeguard, whose name was Kevin, blew his whistle. "Stay near the raft, Jake, or you go back inside the pier."

Jake turned around and headed back to the raft. As he started to climb up, I dove in and swam back toward the shallow water. Jim followed me.

"Let's ask if we can take a canoe out," said Jim. "We can practice paddling."

Kevin pointed to the area on the other side of the pier where the rowboats and canoes were tied up. He said we could practice there as long as we didn't go too far out.

It was very peaceful in the area where the boats were docked. The sand beneath the shallow water was patterned with jagged lines from the lapping waves. Our footsteps stirred the water, causing schools of minnows to dart back and forth around our feet. I closed my eyes and took a deep breath. The smell of the water, the feel of sand beneath my feet, and the gentle slap of the little waves against my legs made me feel happy.

Jim held the canoe while I climbed in and took the front seat. Jim climbed into the back and pushed us away from the dock. A couple of small fish scattered as the canoe slid through the water. Jim paddled skillfully, using the "J" stroke. Though his mother's parents were Native American, he didn't learn how to paddle a canoe from them. He learned from his dad, who was an Eagle Scout and a camp counselor when he was in college.

"There's a turtle," said Jim. "It's a whopper." He turned the bow of the canoe toward the turtle's tail and slid up behind it.

The turtle slid through the water in front of us. Its head was the size of a large orange, and its shell was at least fourteen inches across. It was the biggest turtle I'd ever seen.

I kept my voice low. "A snapper. He's big enough to bite off a finger."

"Or a hand," muttered Jim. "But he'd make good turtle soup."

The turtle paddled away, heading toward the pier. We followed, gliding through the water behind him.

"What if he goes behind the pier?" I asked. "He could bite one of the kids."

Almost as if he'd heard us, the turtle swam under the pier and came out inside the area where the non-swimmers were practicing. Jim whistled to get the lifeguard's attention. The lifeguard climbed down from his perch and walked down the pier toward the turtle. He blew his whistle three times, which was the signal to grab your buddy's hand and come up out of the water.

"Everybody move to the left, please," he shouted. "Stay away from the turtle."

The turtle swam under the pier again and headed back out toward deeper water. The lifeguard blew his whistle to signal that everyone could start swimming again. Jim and I continued to practice paddling. At the end of the week, we would be taking the canoes to Fish Island for an overnight, and we wanted to be ready.

Everyone looked forward to the Fish Island campout. We would cook our dinner over the fire and sleep out under the stars. We would roast hotdogs and marshmallows, and make S'mores for dessert. We had to pack tents, too, in case the weather was cold or rainy. Everyone would learn how to put them up. It was a good time to practice our camping skills.

About twenty minutes later, Kevin blew his whistle again. The swim period was over, and it was time to get out of the water. The turtle was still between the raft and the pier. Jake dove from the raft and swam toward the turtle. The turtle turned and swam toward the lifeguard tower. Jake followed, swimming up behind it. If Jake tried to grab it, the big turtle would bite him. He could lose a finger trying to catch that thing.

I waved to the lifeguard and pointed toward Jake, who was now only a few feet from the snapper.

Kevin blew his whistle and pointed at the turtle. "Snapper," he called. "Stay to the right, Parma. Don't go near it."

"I'm not afraid of turtles," yelled Jake. He swam two more strokes, collided with the turtle, and smacked its shell with his hand. Then he reached out and grabbed the turtle's leg. Even thirty yards away, I could see that turtle's long neck stretching out from the shell and its wide open mouth aiming for Jake's arm. The turtle's head twisted. Its mouth clamped down on Jake's hand. Jake screamed, a loud and terrible shriek that echoed across the lake.

Kevin slid down from the tower and grabbed a paddleboard. Jake was yelling and holding up a bloody hand. The water between the pier and the raft was deep, well over his head. He sank beneath the surface and came up again, thrashing wildly. He screamed again, ending with a gurgle as he sank back under the water. Kevin swam the short distance, dove, and pulled Jake to the surface. He dragged Jake across the paddleboard and pushed it toward the shore. Jim and I pulled our canoe up onto the beach and yelled to the rest of the swimmers to grab their buddies and come out of the water. They all moved fast, and soon no one was in the water but Jake and the lifeguard. The turtle swam just outside the pier, as if it were watching.

Jake stood up from the water, his hand dripping blood. Kevin told him to sit down. He wrapped a big towel around Jake's shoulders, and a smaller one around his hand. In minutes the small towel was red with blood. Kevin asked me to get the first aid kit from the tower. He glanced at the rest of the kids, who stood around watching.

He spoke to someone on the phone, then looked up at me. "Is everybody out of the water?"

"Everyone," I said. "I counted them."

"Is there anything else you want us to do?" asked Jim. "Jake's hand looks pretty bad."

"I've called the nurse," said Kevin. "She'll be down here in a minute. You two can go on up."

I stood next to them, wondering if I should say anything to Jake. Maybe I could tell him I was sorry he was bitten. It served him right, but I wasn't going to say that.

Jake narrowed his eyes and glared at me. "No animal is going to make a fool out of me," he said. Shivers went down my back. I'd heard that comment before.

Kevin waved for us to go on up to camp. As we left I heard Kevin say, "That turtle wasn't trying to make a fool out of you, Jake. It bit you because you provoked it. This is a bad gash, but it could have taken off part of your hand. If I were you, I'd stay away from snapping turtles from now on." Behind his back, Jake gave us the finger with his left hand.

That evening I gave Levi the eagle feathers I'd plucked from under my arm. I told him I'd found them near the bathhouse. It wasn't too far from the truth.

"Wow!" Levi squinted, holding a feather up. "This is from a bald eagle. I've never seen one around here. We should watch for a nest while we're hiking tomorrow."

I didn't say anything. We probably weren't going to find any eagles' nests, but I didn't want to ruin the fun he was having thinking about it.

"How long is the hike?" asked Bill. "I'm not sure Jake is up to it."

"Five or six miles." Levi took out his phone. "I'll text the nurse. If she says he should rest, we'll excuse him from the walk."

"Did he need stitches?" I asked.

Bill nodded. "I think so. They were in the emergency room for a long time."

I knew I should feel sorry for Jake, but I didn't have it in me. He'd brought the injury on himself by messing with a snapping turtle. A big snapping turtle. Stupid.

Terry brought the other Warrior campers to the campfire circle to give us our instructions for the next day's hike. "Cook will have lunches ready for us tomorrow morning," he said. "After breakfast, pick up a lunch bag and two bottles of water. Put them in your backpack. You'll also need sunscreen, insect repellant, and a hat. Wear sturdy shoes—no sandals or flip-flops. Bring a notebook and a pen. We'll start out right after breakfast. We'll climb to the top of Rock Hill and eat our lunch there."

Getting ready for bed was the reverse of getting dressed in the morning. I waited until all the other guys were ready for bed. Then I took the bag that held my shower supplies and pajamas to the boys' bathhouse. I checked the back of my arms in the mirror. There were six or eight bruises, all blue and green and yellow. I didn't think Jake would pinch me again, but if he did, maybe I'd have to take him somewhere and teach him a lesson. A couple of straight punches ought to do it. I closed my eyes and pictured him cowering in the grass, holding his chin and putting up a hand to keep me from hitting him again.

Who was I kidding? He outweighed me by about thirty pounds, and I wasn't good at fighting. Besides, fighting would get us both thrown out of camp. I'd have to find another way to make him stop bullying me.

Maybe the turtle had taken care of Jake for me. The snapper bit the first two fingers on Jake's right hand, and Jake was right-handed. He wouldn't be pinching me with that hand; not for a while, anyway.

As I lifted my arms to put on my pajama top, I noticed something different. The soft white feathers under my arms had grown. They were about an inch long now, and they extended further down the inside of my arm. When had that happened? They'd stayed the same length for several months. Now, in just one day, they'd grown about an inch. My heart started to pound. How was I going to cover these feathers? They'd stick out under a short-sleeved tee shirt. One pair of my pajamas had long sleeves, but I'd need a long-sleeved shirt in the morning—and every day of camp. Did I have a clean long-sleeved shirt for the hike? Some of my clothes were still drying on the clothesline outside.

Back in the cabin, I sorted through the clothes in my suitcase and found two long-sleeved shirts. Those shirts and my jacket were the only long-sleeved things I had with me. Maybe I'd have to write Mom and ask her to send me more clothes. I shoved the suitcase under my bunk and climbed into bed.

That night, I dreamed I climbed the tree on the top of Rock Hill. At the very top of the tree, I found a huge nest. Inside the nest were three baby eagles. I crawled into the nest with them. The mother eagle came back. When she saw me, she began to squawk. She poked me with her beak and shoved me out of the nest. I fell through the air, screaming. Before I hit the ground, I woke up, my heart banging against my ribcage. I shoved hair out of my eyes and took a deep breath. I'd had nightmares before, but this was one of the worst. It took me a long time to get back to sleep.

The next time I woke up, light was streaming across the cabin's wooden floor. Levi was shaking me. "Time to get up, Luke."

I opened my eyes. Jim was already dressed. The other guys had gone to the shower. I pulled my shower bag out from under the bed.

"Get moving," said Levi. "You're going to be late for breakfast."

I pushed the screen door open and went outside. The sun was shining. It was going to be a nice day.

"Want me to wait for you?" asked Jim.

"No, I'll see you at breakfast." I went down the lane into the woods and stopped. I felt the back of my neck prickling, as though someone was watching me. Maybe I should have taken Jim up on his offer to wait. I was asking for trouble, going into the bathhouse alone when the other guys were still around. I stayed behind a tree and watched for them. A few minutes later they came out of the bathhouse and headed back toward the cabin. Inside the bathhouse, I checked all the stalls to make sure they were empty. When I was sure no one else was around, I went into a shower stall and closed the door.

The shower stalls had two sections, divided by a shower curtain. One half was the wet part with the showerhead, and the other half had a bench. There was a hook on the back of the door. I hung my clothes on the hook where they wouldn't get wet, then put my towel on the bench. Turning on the hot water, I stepped into the shower and soaped up. When I was finished, I turned off the water and took my towel from the bench. A hand reached over the shower door and grabbed my clothes. I pounded the hand with my fist. Somebody swore. I slammed the door open, pinning Jake to the next shower stall.

"Drop them, now."

Jake dropped my clothes onto the wet floor. He shoved at the stall's door with his good hand, pushing me backwards. I twisted, trying to catch myself, but slipped and fell, cracking my forehead against the concrete floor. When I sat up, I felt blood running down my head. I reached up to see if there was a gash. Jake was staring at me, wide-eyed. His mouth was open. He wasn't looking at the blood pouring down my face. He was staring at the feathers under my arms.

Chapter Three—Cougar

Jake left the bathhouse in a hurry. This was bad. He'd surely tell the guys what he'd seen. Maybe he'd tell the counselors, or the nurse, or the camp director. Maybe he'd go to the mess hall and announce it to the whole place.

My heart was pounding so hard I couldn't breathe. I took a deep breath and blew it out slowly. I did it again, two more times. When I felt calmer, I tried to think. What if Jake told the counselors I had feathers under my arms? Would they believe him? Probably not. What about the guys? They probably wouldn't believe him either. Still, I didn't like Jake knowing my most private secret. In fact I hated it.

I washed the blood off my face. The cut near the top of my forehead kept oozing. I dabbed at it for a few minutes, but the bleeding didn't stop. Back at the cabin, I rifled through my first aid kit for a bandage. The cut was about an inch long, and the bandage didn't cover it. I'd have to go to the First Aid Office and get a bigger one. This was not good. I didn't want to see the nurse.

The First Aid Office was in the main building, across from the mess hall.

Miss Powell, the nurse, frowned as she examined the cut. "How did you do this?"

"Slipped in the shower."

"Slipped in the shower." She narrowed her eyes as if she didn't believe me.

"Yes."

"Lie down on the cot." Miss Powell peered at me over half-glasses. "I've been a camp nurse for several years now. Campers don't usually slip in the shower. Unless they have a little help, of course."

"I'm clumsy sometimes."

She cleaned the cut, dabbing blood away as she worked. It kept bleeding. She pressed on the cut for a couple of minutes. When she took her hand away, the cut started bleeding again. Finally she pinched the edges together and put three narrow, sticky strips tightly across the edges. Then she loaded crushed ice into a plastic glove to make an ice-pack.

"Hold this over the cut, Luke. The cold will help stop the bleeding."

I held the five-fingered ice-pack against the cut. The ice took away some of the pain. I closed my eyes and leaned my head back against the pillow, feeling better.

"Keep your eyes open," said Miss Powell. "I need to check your pupils." She flashed a light into both of my eyes, then took my pulse.

"You don't have to call the doctor or anything, do you?"

She shook her head. "I don't think so. You've had a tetanus shot, and the cut looks petty clean. You aren't showing any signs of concussion." She lifted the bandage and checked the cut again. The bleeding had stopped. She smoothed anti-biotic cream on it and placed two bandages over it, side by side. "Come back if it starts bleeding again, Luke. No running and no swimming today."

"You're kidding." Swimming was my favorite activity. I was tired of missing it.

Miss Powell crossed her arms and stared at me. "Do I look like I'm kidding?" She wasn't smiling. I shook my head. "Good. If you get a headache or feel like throwing up, let me know right away."

I was late for breakfast. I put scrambled eggs, toast, and orange juice on my tray and sat down next to Jim.

He stared at my forehead. "What happened to you?"

"I slipped in the shower." I glanced around me. Jake and Bill were sitting with a couple of the other guys. Jake eyed me, then stared at his empty plate. The guys were eating and talking just as they always did. Nobody turned to stare at me. No one laughed or whispered to each other. I couldn't believe it. Maybe Jake hadn't told them about my feathers after all. I was glad, but confused too. Jake seemed to get a lot of fun out of teasing and torturing me. Now he had something real to blab around camp. Why hadn't he told them?

Levi came to the table. "The nurse just called me, Luke. She said you can go on the hike if you feel okay. You're supposed to check in with her when we get back. No running, climbing, or swimming."

Great. I might as well be at home.

"As soon as you're finished eating, we'll take off," said Levi. "Don't forget to pick up your lunch and water bottles." He nodded toward a table near the wall that held rows of brown paper lunch bags and a crate of bottled water. Levi went out the front door, and Jake and the other guys followed him.

"Guess what?" Jim was smiling. "Terry found some tracks in the woods last night."

I spread strawberry jam on my toast. "What kind of tracks?"

"He thought it was some kind of cat. He said the tracks were this big." Jim held his hands apart about six inches.

"That's a pretty big track." I wiped a blob of strawberry jam from the front of my shirt. "What do you think it is?"

"I've heard of bobcats in Michigan," said Jim. "Maybe it was a bobcat."

"A bobcat track wouldn't be that big."

"You aren't eating," said Jim. "Does your head hurt?"

"Not really." I put the toast down. I wasn't hungry after all. "We might as well go."

We picked up our lunches and bottled water and headed back to our cabin. I wished I could tell Jim about the feathers. I needed to talk to someone about this, but I was afraid. He'd probably think I was weird. Maybe I was.

Levi, Terry, and the other guys were waiting for us. Levi passed out more water bottles and little packages of mosquito repellant.

"The goal of this nature hike is to identify the types of wildlife that live in the woods," said Terry. "If you see tracks, please call out so we can identify them. If you see an animal, call out quietly or raise your hand. Do not touch or frighten the animal."

We picked up the trail about fifty yards behind the Warrior cabins. The trail was a well-worn path that led through about twenty acres of forest and around the lake to Rock Hill.

Sixteen of us walked single file, following Terry. Levi was at the end of the line. We'd gone about a half mile when we came to a small clearing. Terry held up a hand. We gathered around him.

"Does anyone see any tracks right now?" asked Terry.

I peered at the ground. Twigs and leaves covered the side of the path, but I thought I could see part of a track. I squatted down to brush some leaves away. Sure enough, there were several tracks in the dirt.

"Deer tracks." I pointed at them. When I brushed more leaves away, I saw something very strange. A large track covered most of another deer track. It was the kind of track a cat made—a very large cat. I glanced up at Levi. "There's another track here."

Levi squatted next to me and peered at the track.

"Bobcat?" asked Terry.

Levi shook his head. "Too big."

Jim cleared more leaves and twigs away. Now we could see both the front and hind paw prints. They were at least four feet apart. "I've seen bobcat tracks," said Jim. "These are much bigger. The space between them shows this is a much larger cat."

I nodded. "Looks like cougar, but I've never heard of them coming this far south."

"They roam," said Jim. "They follow the herds. There are a lot of deer in these woods."

For years there had been rumors about panthers in Waterford, a city north of Detroit. The Department of Natural Resources said there were no panthers in Michigan. Then someone found the carcass of a panther that had been hit by a car, so the DNR couldn't deny it anymore. There were panthers in Michigan.

Panther, puma, mountain lion, or cougar—those were different names for the same animal. No one knew where they came from or how many there were. One thing I knew for sure, though. Cougars were carnivores. They'd eat deer, sheep, cattle, and other farm animals. They would also attack and kill people. Shivers ran down my back. A cougar had prowled around on the campgrounds, less than a mile from our cabins. These tracks were fresh. The cougar could be nearby. It could be watching us right now.

Levi took out his cell phone. He turned away and lowered his voice, but I could still hear what he said. "It's at least four or five inches across the pad. It's not a bobcat. Cougar, maybe." He listened for a few seconds. "Everyone's out hiking today. Warriors section A is ahead of us on the trail, and Trackers sections A and B are hiking in the woods on the other side of camp. Someone needs to call them in too." Before he put his phone away, he photographed the tracks. He used one of his sneakers to show the scale of the paw prints.

While Levi was documenting the tracks, I thought about Austin. He was in the Tracker boys' group. When we were trapped in the bodies of animals at the zoo, I'd been very worried about my brother starving to death because he wasn't getting enough to eat. Now I had to worry about him getting eaten by a cougar.

"Will someone notify the Tracker groups?" I asked. I had to make sure Austin was okay.

"The camp director is calling all the counselors," said Levi. "She'll also call the Park Service and the Department of

Natural Resources. They'll have to send somebody out here to find out what made those tracks."

"The tracks look fresh," I said. "The cougar could be pretty close. I thought I could smell him."

"You must have a pretty good sense of smell," said Jim.

I nodded. I didn't tell him I could smell things that were a couple of miles away. It was a trait left over from when I was a Komodo.

We started back toward the camp. Levi waited for me to catch up with him, and we walked side by side. "How come you know so much about animal tracks?" he asked.

"I took a class at the zoo. They showed us a lot of big cat tracks."

"What other tracks can you recognize?" Levi held up his hand to stop the group.

Squatting down, I carefully removed some leaves and twigs from the path. I pointed to a couple of wavy lines in the dirt. "Here's a snake track, or part of one."

Levi grinned. "We should have a class on tracks. You can teach it."

"No thanks." I was still staring at the path. Part of a large cat track was visible near the grassy edge of the trail. A cougar had come here, less than a hundred yards from the Warriors cabins. The track was fresh—probably made sometime in the past three or four hours. It was headed south, toward the woods behind the Tracker cabins.

My mouth went dry. I stared into the woods. Where was that cougar now? Was it anywhere near the Trackers?

Cougars liked to hide in trees. They climbed trees so they could spot prey. When the prey walked under the tree, the cougar would pounce down and kill it. I didn't want a cougar to pounce on my brother—or anyone else. Austin could go grizzly and fight it, but he wouldn't want to morph in front of other people.

I scanned the trees around me, but I couldn't see anything. I needed to get up higher so I could get a better look at the rest of the camp. Grabbing the lowest limb of the tree next to me, I swung myself up. Because I've always been afraid of heights, I didn't usually climb trees. Now I found it easy to climb. I reached for a higher limb, and then another. Soon I was near the top of the tree. I stopped climbing and peered out over the woods.

At first, all I could see were other trees. I squinted, bringing nearby trees and branches into focus. I checked each tree, scrutinizing the lower branches. Squirrels hopped from limb to limb, chasing each other. Birds screamed and fluttered, protecting their nests.

Looking up, I concentrated on longer distances. Soon I could see the blue-gray lake. Shifting my gaze to the right, I spotted the road that led into the camp. On one side of the road, in a large clearing, was the baseball diamond. Beyond the baseball diamond was a large forest we called "Tracker Woods" because it was behind the Tracker cabins. I blinked and narrowed my eyes. Something was moving in the woods. Kids. I refocused again to see them close up. It was the Tracker group, hiking along single file. Austin was third in line.

My heart started to pound. The Trackers were heading further into the woods. Their counselor hadn't heard about the cougar tracks yet. This was dangerous. The cougar could be anywhere in that woods. It could be in a tree right now, waiting to pounce on someone. It might be hunting for prey with two legs, walking upright.

Blinking, I moved my eyes from side to side. I checked every tree in that patch of woods. My eyes caught on movement in a tree. Focusing, I squinted until all I could see was that tree. There it was! A large, tan-colored animal crept slowly along a thick branch. As I watched, the big cat stopped and looked down. Its tail flicked. It stood very still, the big blond head still bent towards the ground. Austin's group was about a quarter mile away. They were heading straight for the tree where the cougar was hiding.

I climbed down quickly and jumped to the ground. The counselors and the other guys were all staring at me.

Levi frowned. "You're in trouble, Luke. Miss Powell said you weren't to climb trees."

"The Trackers are hiking in the woods on the other side of the camp, Levi." My throat was dry and I could hardly get the words out. "They're about halfway between the road and the baseball diamond. They're heading west. The cougar is in a tree about a quarter mile in front of them. You have to call and turn them around! Hurry!"

Terry frowned as though he thought I was nuts. "You couldn't have seen them from here, Luke. The lake is over a mile away. And the baseball diamond is at least a mile from here, too."

We didn't have time for this. In minutes those Trackers would be walking under the tree where the cougar was hiding.

"Please, just call them," I pleaded. "Have them turn around and go back the way they came." I lowered my voice. "Terry, this is a big cat. Those kids could get hurt. We can't take any chances."

Terry let out a long breath, as if he was agreeing with me just to get me off his back.

"Okay. They should get out of the woods anyway." He pressed some numbers on his cell phone, and then walked away so I couldn't hear what he said. Levi was still staring at me like I had two heads.

I took a deep breath and looked up at the tree I'd just climbed. It was almost fifty feet tall. That was as tall as a five-story building. Had I really climbed to the top of it? I'd always been afraid of heights, but I'd just climbed a tree that was five stories tall. How could I have seen something that was two miles away? It was impossible for a human.

But I wasn't totally human. I was ninety percent human and ten percent eagle. My eyes had become as sharp as an eagle's eyes. Was that ten percent taking over my body? Was it going to turn into twenty percent? Fifty percent? Were my feet going to turn into talons? Was I going to grow feathers all over my body? I couldn't let that happen. As soon as we got back to camp, I was going to borrow a phone and call Gramps.

My grandfather was smart. He taught astronomy and astrophysics at the college in our town. When Austin and I had turned into zoo animals the previous fall, Gramps found a way to help us become human again. He'd know how to help me now.

Terry's phone rang. He put it to his ear and listened, then smiled and gave me a "thumbs up" signal. He thanked the caller and put the phone back in his pocket.

"That was the Trackers' counselor," he explained. "They've turned the kids around and they're on their way back to camp."

The hairs on the back of my neck prickled. Slowly, I turned around. The boys had gathered in a semicircle around me. Every one of them was staring at me. Jake muttered something to Bill. Bill's mouth fell open. Bill whispered to the guy next to him. I knew what they were saying. Jake must have told Bill about my feathers, and now Bill was telling everyone else. I heard someone mutter the word "freak."

I hated that word. It meant I was different. Odd. I didn't belong in their group. They were right. None of them were my friends. Jim was my friend, though. He would be my friend no matter what I looked like.

Terry blew his whistle. "Listen up, guys. Here's the new plan. The camp director says no one is allowed in the woods until the sheriff tells us it's safe. We have two choices: arts and crafts in the mess hall or waterfront activities."

Everyone began to talk at once. No one seemed happy about going to arts and crafts class. Terry blew his whistle again. "We're going back to the cabins. Then we'll change into swimsuits and practice paddling the canoes. No one is to go off on their own, not even to the bathroom." He started back down the path toward our cabins. The group followed. Jim and I were near the end of the line. Jake and Bill were behind us.

"This is lame," said Jake. "Just because stupid bird boy thinks he saw a cougar."

"It was probably just a coyote or something," said Bill.

Jim turned around to face them. "It wasn't a coyote. Those tracks were made by some kind of a big cat. A coyote's tracks are more like a dog's."

Jake made bird call sounds. Then he yelled "Bird boy!" He slid close behind me and pinched my arm, hard. I turned fast and knocked his hand aside with my fist. Then I saw the white bandage on Jake's right hand. Apparently he could pinch just as hard with his left hand.

Levi yelled at him. "Jake! Stop right there. You too, Luke." He waited until the rest of the group had gone further down the path. Then he pointed at Jake. "I saw you pinch Luke. I've told you before about bullying. We don't tolerate physical abuse of any kind at this camp."

"I didn't mean to hurt him." Jake laughed and slapped me on the back. "I was just kidding around. It's no big deal, right, Luke?" He grinned at me, showing a mouthful of teeth. Some of them were pointed, like a wolf's fangs. I didn't say anything.

"Let me see that arm, Luke." Before I could stop him, Levi pushed my sleeve up almost to my elbow. The feathers were higher up, so he didn't see them. But he did see the bruises I'd been trying to hide.

"The whole side of your arm is black and blue," said Levi. "Did Jake do this?"

Jake narrowed his eyes at me. I kept my mouth shut. I wasn't afraid of Jake, but it wouldn't take long for a doctor to find my feathers.

"It's nothing. Don't worry about it. I fell and hit my arm on a log." I tried to pull my sleeve down over the bruises.

"Let's get back to camp," said Levi. "We'll talk about this later." Then he stopped and rested a restraining hand on Jake's arm. "This isn't over. I'll be reporting today's abuse of a fellow camper to the director. If I ever see you touch Luke—or anybody else—again, you'll go straight home. We'll also report it to the police. Got that?"

Jake pulled his arm away. "Keep your hands off me or my lawyer will hear about it." He poked Levi in the chest. "My father will have you fired." Then Jake stalked down the path after the other guys.

When we reached our cabin, I asked Levi if I could be excused from paddling the canoes today. "I'm not supposed to get this dressing wet," I explained.

Levi glanced at the cabin. "I'll excuse you from the activity, but you have to stay in the mess hall or the nurse's office. You can't be alone in your cabin."

"Can I stay with him?" asked Jim.

"I think that's a good idea," said Levi. "You could walk to the mess hall together."

Jim went inside the cabin and got some money for both of us. When he came back out, we started down the path toward the Trading Post.

"You didn't really find those feathers near the bathhouse, did you," asked Jim. His tone told me he already knew the answer.

I stared at him. "How long have you known?"

"I saw the feathers one night when you were asleep," said Jim. "You had your arm over your head, and your sleeve was up. That's why I didn't report Jake for pinching you, even though he's a jerk. I figured you wouldn't want to be examined."

As we walked, I told Jim how I had plucked the feathers from my skin. "It was hard work," I said. "And it hurt."

"It would be very painful for you to pluck them," said Jim. "And it would take a long time. A bald eagle has about seven thousand feathers."

We had reached the camp store, which was just outside the mess hall. The camp store was built like a little log cabin, with a sign outside that said "Trading Post." Inside there were shelves of sweatshirts and tee-shirts with the camp logo printed on the front. Purple rain ponchos for the girls and green ones for the boys were displayed on a rack of hangers. Next to the counter was a freezer full of Popsicles, ice cream bars, and orange sherbet cups, as well as shelves of other goodies. But now my stomach felt queasy, and I wasn't hungry anymore. I sat down on the long bench on the porch of the Trading Post. Jim sat next to me.

"You probably think I'm pretty weird," I said.

Jim shrugged. "I'm part Native American, remember? Many of our people believe in shapeshifters."

"Do you think I'm a shapeshifter?"

"I just watched you climb to the top of a fifty-foot tree in under a minute. Then you spotted your brother and that cougar when they were both almost two miles away. You have eyesight like an eagle. You go to high places like an eagle. You have—"

"Feathers like an eagle." I finished the sentence for him. "If I was a shapeshifter, wouldn't I turn all the way into an eagle?"

Jim smiled at me. "Maybe you will."

"I already have. Once, anyway. It's a long story."

"We have a lot of time," said Jim. "I'd like to hear it."

"I don't want the other guys to know."

Jim nodded. "You got it."

So I told him the whole story, starting with that terrible day when Austin and I were turned into zoo animals. He listened quietly. He didn't look surprised or shocked. He was as calm as if all of his friends could turn into animals.

"After we became human again, both of us had animal traits for a while. It took another trip to the zoo to straighten us out." I paused. "Almost. I still have some Komodo traits. I have some eagle traits, too, besides the feathers."

"You probably saved a couple of lives today with those eagle traits," said Jim. "Can you still become a Komodo? I'd love to see that." He grinned at me.

"I hope you never do. The Komodo is dangerous. I'm always afraid I'll hurt someone when I'm in that form. I haven't turned into a Komodo since we left the zoo."

"What happens to your clothes when you turn into an animal?" asked Jim. "Do you still have them when you morph back?"

"I'm not sure what happens to them while we're in animal form," I answered. "But when we become human again, we're wearing the same clothes we had on before we morphed."

"What about Austin?" Jim leaned forward with his elbows on his knees. "You said he turned into a grizzly bear. Does he have any bear traits now?"

I shrugged. "I haven't seen any."

Then I remembered something. When Mom wanted a chair moved in the living room, it usually took two of us. Last week Austin had picked up a heavy chair and carried it across the room like it was a box of crackers. That didn't mean he still had grizzly bear traits, did it? He was probably just growing. Probably.

Chapter Four—Missing Trackers

I watched as Levi and Terry walked down the path toward the Trading Post. Both of them looked worried. Levi had his cell phone next to his ear.

"How long has she been missing?" He listened for a few seconds. "That's the section of woods where one of my kids saw the cougar. Cougar. Mountain lion. They're the same animal. Yes, I do believe him. This kid knows animals, and he's good with tracks."

The two counselors stopped next to us, and Levi spoke into his phone again. "We're coming now. I'll bring Luke with me. Luke Brockway. He can show us exactly where he saw the cat."

Levi hung up and turned to me. "You'll need to come with us, Luke. One of the younger campers got separated from her group and is lost. They think she's somewhere in the woods, maybe in the area where you saw the cougar. Do you think you could find that place again?"

I jumped up from the bench. "Sure. I know right where it is. Can Jim come too?"

We piled into one of the camp Jeeps and drove past the baseball field to the edge of the woods where I'd seen the cougar. Terry parked the Jeep on the side of the road, and we started down the path where the Trackers had been hiking. I led the way, with Jim right behind me and the counselors following.

Levi's phone rang again. He listened for a few seconds and then asked, "Why do we need the sheriff?" He glanced at Terry, shaking his head, then replaced the phone in a pouch on his belt.

"What was that all about?" asked Terry.

"Now two kids are missing from the Trackers section," said Levi. "And there's more bad news. Someone spotted a bear. A grizzly bear. The camp director has called in the county sheriff."

Terry laughed. "There are no grizzly bears in Michigan. There are black bears up north, but not down here."

"Yesterday we didn't think there were cougars in our woods either," said Levi. "Now we've seen the tracks. Who knows what other kind of animal will be around tomorrow?"

Jim and I glanced at each other. I shook my head, feeling sick. I was pretty sure I knew the bear. It had to be Austin, but why would he morph? He'd hated being a bear during our time at the zoo. Neither of us had changed form since the day Dunn Nikowski died in the zoo parking lot. Now the county sheriff had been called in, and he'd be bringing a gun. If my brother was still in the form of a bear, he could get shot. I had to find that bear before anyone else did. To do that, I had to get up high again. From the top of a tree I could scan the woods pretty well.

I raised my hand to signal everyone to stop. Placing one hand on the limb of the tree nearest me, I swung myself up.

"Brockway, get down here before you fall." Terry glared up at me, hands on his hips.

"Let him be," Levi muttered. "He knows what he's doing."

I climbed higher in the tree, being careful to choose branches that were thick enough to hold me. Finally I was high enough to see the branches of trees about a quarter of a mile away. I narrowed my eyes until my vision changed from human to eagle. It was almost like looking through binoculars. Soon I spotted little bugs crawling along a nearby branch. Three tiny birds peeked out from a nest. They were thin and kind of ugly. I changed focus so I could see a wider area.

I focused on the trees about two hundred yards away, where the Trackers had been hiking today. That was where I'd seen the cougar. Moving my gaze from tree to tree, I watched for the big cat.

Then I saw it. The tawny blond body of the cougar stretched along a limb, its color easily visible among the green and black hues of the trees. It was about six feet long from head to tail and must have weighed about two hundred pounds. The big cat moved slowly, its head down as though it was stalking something tasty on the ground. Then it froze. It stood still as a statue on the limb, about ten feet above the ground. The blond tail flicked, and the huge head bent as if ready to dive.

It happened again, just as it had with the wolves at the zoo. I sensed the animal's thoughts. Or maybe I sensed its feelings. However it happened, I became aware that the cat was hungry. There was another, more urgent reason she had to hunt. An image of two cougar cubs bloomed into my mind. They were tiny, with black spots on their tan fur. The cougar was female, and she had babies to feed.

I squinted, my eyes following the direction of the cougar's gaze. My heart skipped a beat! For a few seconds I was so terrified I couldn't breathe. On the ground beneath the tree was a red-haired girl. Megan! She sat with her back against the tree trunk, staring up at the cougar. She didn't move or speak. Her mouth was frozen open as though she had tried to scream and couldn't get it out. The cougar stood on the thick limb above her, staring downward. Its twitching tail went still.

"Megan!" My mouth and throat had gone dry, and the word came out in a squeak. I slid down the tree, my muscles quivering, my skin feeling the prick of scales. The deadly realization had already dawned on me. As an eagle, the cougar would take me. I couldn't turn Komodo fast enough to help her. Even if I transformed in a nanosecond and ran as fast as a Komodo could, the cougar would reach Megan before I did. I was still almost two hundred yards away. It would take me about half a minute to reach her, but the cougar could reach her in a two-second pounce.

A gigantic brown shape loomed into view on the far side of the baseball field. Its head drew level with the tree limb where the cougar crouched. A grizzly bear! The bear's paws were raised in a karate strike position. It had to be Austin. There weren't any grizzlies in Michigan, and definitely no grizzly bears that knew karate.

The strange quivering I'd felt all over my body died away. I took a deep breath to calm myself. The eagle couldn't help Megan, but the Komodo could. I wouldn't morph unless I had to, but before I could do anything I had to get closer. Using the Komodo's speed, I darted from tree to tree, trying to find a good position to help Megan. When I reached a thick maple tree that was close to her, Levi spotted me.

He shouted for me to get back. From where he stood, he could see the bear and probably the cougar, but he couldn't see Megan on the ground beneath the tree. He didn't know she was in danger. The cougar could reach her with quick leap from the tree. The grizzly bear was in front of her, only a step away. If it stepped backwards, the seven-hundred-fifty-pound bear would flatten Megan. I had to get her out of there. As soon as the animals moved away, I'd pull her out of the fight area.

The cougar screeched and swiped a paw at the bear. The bear smacked back, hitting the big cat's shoulder. The cougar flew off the limb and landed several feet from the tree. It rolled over on the ground, then quickly bounced back up on its legs and snarled at the bear. Hunching, the grizzly opened its mouth and growled. Then it moved directly in front of Megan, shielding her from the cougar. I moved closer. I was now only a couple of yards from the tree. As soon as the bear stepped away, I'd grab Megan and pull her to safety.

The cat backed up, but not far enough. The bear smacked it again. The cougar rolled about ten yards before getting back up. The bear followed it, ready for another hit.

I put my arms under Megan and pulled her backwards and away from the tree.

"Ow! With a cry of pain, Megan clenched one arm against her chest and tried to stand. I pulled her against me, dragging her away from the two fighting animals. When we were far enough away, I gently lowered her to a sitting position. She was breathing hard, and her face was pale and sweaty. She still held one arm close to her body, as if protecting it. I could see a large purple bruise blooming close to her elbow.

The cougar circled, snarling. Blood dripped from scratches on its head. The bear roared again. The cougar turned and ran into the woods. The bear followed, crashing through the brush behind it.

Terry and Levi pushed through the tangled branches to where Megan and I waited. Both counselors were pale and out of breath.

"Brockway! What's the matter with you?" Levi's voice was hoarse. "You could have been killed by either one of those animals."

"I had to get her out of there, Levi. She could have been killed."

Levi glanced at Megan as if seeing her for the first time. "You must be one of the missing Trackers."

Terry squatted down next to Megan. "What happened? Did you hurt your arm?"

Megan winced as Terry touched her arm. "I tripped and fell. I hit my arm on a rock."

"Let's put it in a sling," said Levi. "Then we'll take you to the nurse."

We walked back to the Jeep, with Terry and Levi supporting Megan between them. Terry sorted through the first aid kit and found a white triangle of material. Levi slipped it under Megan's arm and tied the ends around her neck. Then he and Terry helped her into the Jeep. I slid in next to her.

"Will Austin be all right?" whispered Megan. She knew the bear was Austin. "The sheriff will have a gun."

"I know." I was worried too.

Terry and Levi got into the Jeep. "We have to get out of here, fast. That was a grizzly bear," said Levi. "They kill people."

"What about the other Tracker?" I asked. "We can't leave him out here. You said the sheriff is coming. He'll be armed."

"You kids are going back to camp," said Levi. "I know you meant well, Luke, but you didn't use good judgment getting that close. Either of those animals could have gone after you."

"I wasn't going to stand there and do nothing," I answered. "Megan could have been hurt."

I didn't want to go back to camp. Once Austin morphed back into a boy, he'd have an angry cougar to deal with. But if he stayed in his grizzly bear form, the sheriff might shoot him. Either way, he'd be in bad trouble. I had to find my brother before the cougar or the sheriff did.

It was too late. The sheriff's car pulled up behind us. Two men in tan uniforms got out of the cruiser and strode toward the Jeep. One of them carried a rifle. The counselors got out of the Jeep and went to meet them.

"I understand you kids saw some animals out here," said the sheriff

"We saw a grizzly bear," said Terry. "At least seven or eight hundred pounds."

The sheriff smirked. "Are you sure it was a grizzly? No grizzlies in this area. Black bears up north. No grizzlies."

"It was a grizzly." Levi's tone was sharp. "It fought with the cougar. Both of them were close to us—not even thirty yards from here. They ran off in that direction." He pointed into the woods.

"Mountain lions don't usually come this far south," said the sheriff. "A grizzly bear and a cougar." He shook his head.

"Maybe the circus is in town," said the deputy. The corner of his mouth went up in a sneer. I could tell he thought we were all crazy.

"Let me show you the tracks," I said, stepping out of the Jeep.

The sheriff reached out and touched the bandage on my forehead. "What happened to you?"

"I fell in the bathhouse. Sheriff, you have to listen to me. There's another camper missing in the woods. If you go out there and start shooting, you could hit him by accident."

"We'll be very careful." He glanced into the woods. "Now, I want you to show me the exact place where you saw the bear."

"Back here." I waved for him to follow and headed for the tree where the bear and cougar fought. "There are tracks here," I said, pointing at a clear set of four large cougar tracks.

"Something has certainly churned up this dirt." The sheriff stepped on several of the tracks, smearing them.

I found the place where the cougar rolled into the brush. "Here's where they fought," I said, pointing to the ground. "See the cougar tracks?"

The sheriff bent over to look. The cougar tracks were clear if you could get your head down close enough to see them. He was kind of thick around the middle, so he couldn't bend very far.

I pushed some leaves away. "More tracks here. And here's where she rolled."

"She?" He glanced back toward Megan. "Did that animal hurt that little girl?"

"No, the cougar is female."

"Is that so?" He stared at me, frowning. "Male or female, it's a dangerous animal and we can't have it around here where there are people."

"Do you have to shoot it? Couldn't you catch it and take it up north or somewhere?" That cougar had babies to take care of, but I didn't want to explain that to the sheriff.

"Hey!" A familiar voice called out from the direction of the woods.

"It's my brother!" I trotted down the path to meet Austin, who had a couple of scratches on the side of his face.

"Glad you're back safe, young man," said the sheriff. He patted Austin on the back. "How did you get separated from your group?"

Austin lowered his voice, but I still heard him. "I had a bladder emergency, sir."

The sheriff nodded. Then he turned to Levi and Terry. "As soon as a couple of other deputies get here, we'll start tracking those animals. Keep all the kids out of the woods for now. We'll let you know when it's safe."

Levi took a map from the Jeep's glove compartment and spread it out over the hood of the Jeep. The two counselors, the sheriff, and his deputy gathered around it.

"This camp covers about three hundred acres," said Levi, running his finger around the map. "This area is all woods. Where the camp's acreage ends, there's a nature preserve and a couple of dairy farms."

"Dairy farms? That cougar will head right for the cattle," said the sheriff. "The bear—or whatever it was—might too."

"It was a bear, Sheriff. A grizzly," said Levi in a tight voice.

The sheriff clasped Levi's shoulder. "Get these young-sters to safety. I'll call for backup. We'll keep in touch." He folded the map and put it in his pocket.

"These kids need to see the nurse," said Terry. "Let's get going."

We sped away, leaving the sheriff and his deputy behind to carry out their hunt. They wouldn't find the bear, although there would be a lot of confusing tracks. I hoped they wouldn't find the cougar either. Maybe she'd go back where she came from. From what I'd read, cougars weren't native to this area of Michigan. Most predators followed their prey, and there were a lot of deer in these woods. This cougar was probably just passing through our camp on her way to somewhere else. Still, she was a big cat and she had to eat so she could feed her babies. It was better not to get in her way in case she had a taste for a human-burger.

We went over a bump, and Megan moaned. She hugged her injured arm closer to her body.

"What happened to you, Megan?" I whispered.

"She fell backwards over a fallen tree," said Austin. "Un-fortunately the tree had an occupant."

Megan sighed. "I'm not usually that clumsy." She patted Austin's hand. "Thank heavens you were there. That cougar would have had me for lunch."

Levi glanced at us over his shoulder. "Do you think you broke your arm?"

"I don't think so. I didn't feel anything snap." Megan closed her eyes.

"It hurts a lot, doesn't it," I whispered, patting her good arm.

"Of course it hurts," snapped Austin.

I blinked. Austin sounded angry. Maybe he was upset because he'd morphed into a bear again. As soon as we were alone I'd have to ask him how that happened.

Then I remembered the feeling I had when I spotted that cougar on the tree limb. Megan was on the ground beneath the tree. I was seconds away from transforming into a Komodo, even with the counselors standing nearby. Austin didn't care who saw him. He'd turned grizzly bear to protect Megan.

We pulled up in front of the building where the First Aid Office was located. Megan, Austin, and I went inside. Miss Powell, the nurse, looked up from a crossword puzzle she was working on. She glanced at my head, then at Megan's arm, then at the scratches on Austin's face.

"Who's the patient?" she asked.

"She is," Austin and I said together. We were both pointing at Megan.

"Then I think you gentleman can go out and I'll take it from here. Luke, come back here after lunch. I need to check that cut on your head. Austin, make sure you clean those scratches. Maybe you'd better come back with Luke."

I told Austin I wasn't hungry and headed for the Warrior section of the camp. As soon as I stepped into the cabin, the hairs on the back of my neck prickled. The air was heavy with danger. From the side of my eye, I saw Jake raise his arms. The others were just behind him. I tore out of the cabin, slamming the screen door against it and nearly hitting Jake in the face. I ran as fast as I could to get away, heading toward the woods. The sound of their tramping feet echoed in my ears. All four of them were after me! What were they going to do to me?

The glands in the back of my mouth began to water, and claws stabbed at the insides of my fingers. I wanted to turn into that strong, dangerous animal and send them all shrieking away. But I fought the urge to morph. No matter what happened, I couldn't go Komodo. Not here. Not in front of the guys.

They were breathing hard, gaining on me, ready to pound me into stew. My toe caught in a branch and my face smashed into the ground. I got a mouthful of dirt. I pushed myself up again.

Something dark fell over my head. Arms came around my legs in a football tackle. I went down again, smashing into something sharp. Bodies piled on top of me, shoving me harder against the sharp point of a branch. Cloth covered my face, and somebody was on top of the cloth. I couldn't breathe. I kicked and shoved, but I couldn't get free. My back scraped against a rock. I tried to roll out from under them and hit my head on a log.

"Pull up his shirt!" yelled Jake.

"Leave him alone!" It was Jim's voice. His words were muffled, as if someone had put a hand over his mouth. Scuffling noises added to the din. Something crashed into the dirt near me.

"Shut up, Indian. Go ahead, pull it up!" yelled Jake. "I'm not lying. See for yourself."

"What's going on here?" It was Austin's voice.

"Get lost, punk," said Jake.

"Oof!" Something heavy hit the ground.

"I said let him go." Austin's voice was deadly calm.

Someone swore, saying the F word.

Thump! Whomp! Screech! Twigs and branches snapped around me. It sounded like three wrestling matches going on at the same time.

Suddenly my arms and legs were free. A weight lifted from my back, and the cover was pulled from my face. I could breathe again. I could see, too. I shoved hair out of my eyes and looked around. Bodies littered the ground. Jake rolled over, moaning. Bill had a bloody lip. Matt was rubbing his head. Jerry was doubled up near a fallen log.

Austin held out a hand. I took it and he pulled me up as if I weighed ten pounds. "You okay, Luke? Your head is bleeding again."

I felt my head. The bandage was wet. When I took my hand away, my fingers were covered with blood. "Great. I guess I'd better go see Miss Powell again and get a clean bandage."

"I'll go with you," said Austin.

"Me too," said Jim. He picked himself up from the ground and brushed dirt from his arms.

"Are you going to tell the counselors?" asked Bill. He looked worried. "We'll be in big trouble."

"That's what you deserve," said Austin.

"No way!" said Matt. "We weren't going to hurt him."

"We just wanted to see if he had feathers," said Jerry.

"That sounds intelligent. I can't wait to hear what the director will say when you tell her that," said Austin. "Or what the judge says when our parents sue you." Leaving them behind, the three of us headed to the First Aid Office.

Austin glanced at me as we walked. "What are you going to tell the nurse?" We stopped walking for a minute to get our stories straight.

"I can't tell her about the guys tackling me." I winced as I tried to think. My head hurt and I felt a little dizzy. "She'll want to have me checked over by the doctor. I have to avoid that." I glanced at Jim. "You know why."

"Does he know about the feathers?" asked Austin.

I stared at my brother. "You know?"

Austin smiled. "I've always known. That's why I insisted on coming to camp with you. I was afraid something like this would happen."

I blew out a long breath. My ribs were hurting. I didn't tell Austin or Jim, but I'd hit the jagged end of that fallen tree when Jake knocked me to the ground. The hard, sharp edge of the wood had jabbed the space between my ribs. I hoped it hadn't broken one of them. That would mean an X-ray, and a closer check by the doctor. I decided not to mention my sore ribs to the nurse.

When we arrived at the First Aid Office, Megan had gone to lunch. Miss Powell gave me a washcloth and told me to wash my face and hands with soap and water. Then she cleaned the cut on my head and put fresh bandages on it. She made me lie down on the cot in the corner and said I had to stay there for a half hour.

"I'm getting hungry," said Austin. "Jim and I can go eat. Should we bring you something?"

"I'm not hungry." I closed my eyes and listened to the door closing behind them.

My head hurt. My chest hurt where I'd hit the jagged edge of the tree. It hurt every time I took a deep breath. I had painful scrapes on my elbows and knees. Anger roiled up in me—anger at Jake and his friends. I was angry with Jake for bullying me and pinching me until I ached all over. I was furious with all of them for attacking me and knocking me down, blinding me with a blanket. I was angry with myself as well. I should have dealt with Jake differently, right from the start. I couldn't report what he'd done because I didn't want the nurse to check me and find the feathers. But I could have asked Austin for help. Or Jim. Or an adult who wasn't connected with the camp. Like Gramps.

When Austin and I were living as zoo animals, Gramps had helped us deal with a bully much worse than Jake—Dunn Nikowski. Dunn was a temporary night guard at the zoo. He used a cattle prod—a metal thing that uses electricity to stun whatever it touches—to show big animals that he was the boss. He turned it on me when I was a Komodo dragon. He used it on Austin too. I felt angry all over again just thinking about it.

Jake reminded me of Dunn, though their faces didn't look the same. But he stood the way Dunn stood, with his arms crossed and rocking back and forth on his heels. And he was a bully too, just like Dunn.

It was time for a do-over. Gramps always told me that we couldn't go back and make a brand new start, but we could start from now and make a brand new ending. Thanks to Austin, I had a chance for a new ending with the guys in my cabin. I wasn't going to take any more abuse. If Jake touched me, I'd knock his hand away. I'd tell the counselor he had tried to pinch me again but I'd grabbed his hand and stopped him. If I said that, I wouldn't have to be checked by Miss Powell. They'd call the police. That would be the end of Jake's days at this camp.

Making a plan made me feel better, but I still felt angry. Four guys had attacked me, all at once. Just thinking about it made me want to clobber them all. As a Komodo, I could deal with them. They wouldn't be able to get away from me, because Komodo dragons can run twelve miles an hour, much faster than most humans. It wouldn't do any good for them to dive into the water, because a Komodo can swim. Even climbing a tree wouldn't help, unless they got up pretty high. The Komodo could stand on his hind legs and reach them. Maybe even climb a little. Just one little nip by the Komodo would give each guy enough venom to cause pain and require hospital treatment. The problem was, Komodo venom could be deadly. I really didn't want to kill anyone.

Maybe I could become an eagle instead. That would allow me to fly fast and attack. An eagle's talons are sharp and can dig into a small animal and fly away with it. They can drag a big animal a short distance. That would work.

My body began to quiver. My arms and legs trembled, and I felt the prick of scales beneath my skin. Nails stabbed at the inside of my fingers, and my hands itched to turn into claws. Or maybe talons. This wasn't good. I needed to get out of here before Miss Powell noticed what was happening. I couldn't allow myself to turn into an animal. I had to get control.

"I've got to use the bathroom," I said, rolling off the bunk.

I left the First Aid Office and hurried to the bathhouse. My hands were shaking, and it felt like insects were crawling all over my skin. The creepy feeling usually meant I was about to change forms. I took a deep breath to calm myself and stop my animal nature from emerging. It took five breaths—a much longer time than usual—to settle myself down. That was probably because I was now fighting both the Komodo and the eagle forms to keep them from taking over my body.

Thankfully, no one else was in the bathhouse. Leaning against the sink, I washed my hands and dried them with a paper towel. I wiped the water off my forearms and stopped short. The feathers had spread. Downy white feathers extended down the inside of both arms, all the way to my elbows. Glancing at my reflection, I blinked. Blinked again. Pale yellow eyes stared back at me!

Chapter Five—Junior Lifeguard

I'd been through this before. Last fall, after we came home from the zoo, my eyes had turned sort of a golden-amber color. Like the Komodo, I could run fast and smell things that were far away. Though I looked human, I still had some Komodo traits.

Now my eagle abilities were getting stronger. Maybe it was because I'd been using my eagle traits more. I liked using eagle traits. I could see things that were two miles away. Being able to catch Megan when she fell from the zoo's water tower and helping to save her from becoming a cougar's dinner made me feel like a hero. It felt great to help people. The problem was, doing those things caused me to become even more like a bird. Feathers had spread down to my elbows. I had pale yellow eyes like an eagle—which would be hard to hide. What else was going to happen? Was I going to start looking for a nest?

As I left the bathhouse, the breeze blew gently through the trees over my head, rustling the leaves. I huffed out a long breath. I didn't want to be a Komodo dragon or an eagle. I wanted to be human. If I wanted to be human, I had to stop relying on animal qualities. I had to use my human skills and traits before I forgot how.

The giant bell outside the mess hall was clanging. That meant we were all supposed to gather there right away. I hurried to the cabin, sorted through my suitcase for a long-sleeved shirt, and pulled the sleeves down over the feathers. Taking sunglasses to cover my eyes, I hurried back to the mess hall.

Jim and the other guys were already there. No one commented about my sunglasses. They probably thought I had two black eyes from their attack. They didn't look too good either. Bill's lip was swollen, and Matt had a bruise on his cheek.

Mrs. Harris walked to the front of the room. The sheriff was with her. Everyone grew quiet.

"Sheriff Danbury and his deputies have completed their search of the grounds," said Mrs. Harris. "He's going to tell you about it."

The sheriff cleared his throat. "I'm glad to tell you that we didn't find any trace of a bear or a cougar."

"There were tracks," said Levi. "We saw them. We saw the bear, too."

The sheriff nodded. "Yes, there were tracks. We followed them through the woods to the farm on the other side of the camp. We told the farmer about the tracks and that we hadn't seen any bears or cougars. We told him to keep an eye out for these animals and call us if he saw anything." He turned to Mrs. Harris. "We believe it's safe for the campers to resume their normal activities. However, they should stay in groups. Don't let any of them go into the woods alone."

Mrs. Harris thanked the sheriff and then addressed us. "Your parents have all been emailed, texted, or called about the possibility of these animals being on the grounds," she said. "So far no parents have informed me that they are coming to get you early. Not everyone has answered yet, but I'm optimistic you'll all be allowed to stay. I know you're all looking forward to our overnight camping experience on Fish Island. It's a beautiful place, and our campers always love to go there. If it isn't raining, you'll get to sleep outside." Everyone cheered.

Mrs. Harris continued. "Because you missed your hike today, we've scheduled extra swim, boating, riding, and craft sessions before supper. You may choose one activity. Check with your counselors to see if there's space. There will be a maximum of twenty for the water sports." After another round of laughing and cheering, the sheriff shook hands with Mrs. Harris and left. Levi followed him out the door, and I followed Levi.

The sheriff stopped as we approached the cruiser.

"There were cougar tracks, Sheriff," I said. I didn't mean to sound rude. I took a deep breath to calm myself. "You saw them yourself."

Levi rubbed the back of his neck. "I'm telling you, I saw the animals with my own eyes. What about the bear? You think we made that up, too?"

The sheriff sighed. "No one said you made it up. The tracks prove the mountain lion was there." He shook his head and spoke quietly. "Son, I don't know what else to tell you. I've had men out scouring this area for the past twelve hours. We'll keep looking, but whatever was here is gone. We know they have large territories. It could be far away by now. If you see it again, we'll come back."

We watched the sheriff's cruiser pull away. The bear was gone. I knew that for sure. But the cougar was a real animal. It had probably stayed out of the sheriff's way, hiding in the trees under cover of night. I was glad it got away, but I felt bad for the cattle on the farms outside the camp's borders. Sooner or later that cat was going to get a taste for a beef steak. Rare.

Back at the cabin, the guys were changing into their swimsuits. None of them looked at me. I pulled my swimsuit and towel from the clothesline and headed to the bathhouse to change. I left my long-sleeved shirt and sunglasses on.

Jim was waiting for me when I came out. "I put our name on the list for the canoes."

"Thanks." It was great to have a friend like Jim. He had my back.

We followed the long stairway down to the beach, stopping to turn over our tags at the landing. I got into a canoe and went to the front seat, as usual. Jim shoved the canoe into the water, stepping into it as it slid forward. We paddled out about thirty yards, giving other campers room to launch their canoes. Soon we were all in the water. The counselors had taken a canoe out as well.

Jim and I paddled smoothly across the lake, taking our time. I loved the quiet. The only sounds were the light ripples of water and the distant hum of a plane somewhere above the clouds. Ahead of us, a fish leapt into the air and splashed back into the lake. Behind us, Jake and Bill turned in a circle. Jake wasn't controlling the direction of the canoe very well. He had a big plastic bag over the dressing on his hand, which probably got in the way. The counselors pulled up next to them and spent a couple of minutes demonstrating how to steer.

Then they pulled alongside our canoe, watching us carefully. After a few minutes Terry said, "Good work, guys." As they paddled away, Jake sneered at us.

We practiced for about a half hour, then pulled our canoe up onto the shore. Tracker Group A was waiting for their turn with the canoes. As soon as a canoe came in, the Warriors got out of it and Trackers got in. Jim and I stopped to watch for a few minutes. Megan and her buddy Louise took a canoe out about fifty yards. They were paddling slowly, trying to do the stroke correctly. Another canoe was churning through the water, heading directly toward them. There were two guys in the canoe. They looked like Jake and Bill.

"That canoe is going way too fast," said Jim.

Jake and Bill were leaning forward, pushing the water with their paddles as though they were in some kind of race. They were heading straight for Megan's canoe. If they didn't slow down, they'd ram it broadside!

Waving to the lifeguard and yelling, I ran out on the pier. Too late. Jake's canoe slammed into the girls, tipping the canoe and dumping both girls into the water. Louise's head came up first. Treading water, she brushed wet hair from her eyes and looked around.

"Megan," she cried. "Where are you?" But Megan did not appear.

I grabbed a floating ring from a post. Before I could throw it, someone dove off the end of the pier and swam toward the overturned canoe. He swam fast, with strong, skillful strokes. The lifeguard grabbed a paddleboard and dove in also. He was several strokes behind the first swimmer.

Megan's head bobbed up out of the water. She flailed her arms wildly, but she wasn't swimming. Then she sank under the water again. It looked as though she didn't know how to swim! If someone didn't save her she would drown!

The two swimmers had reached the overturned canoe. One was the swimmer who dove off the pier first, and the other was the lifeguard, Kevin. They dove under the water near the canoe. We couldn't see what they were doing. Everyone was very quiet, watching for them to come up again. After a minute Kevin and the other swimmer came up for air. I squinted, trying to see who the first swimmer was. Both of them took a deep breath and dove back under the water again. What were they doing? Why couldn't they find Megan?

My heart pounded as I watched them. I felt the prick of scales under my skin. Komodos could swim. If I had to go Komodo to save Megan, I would. Jake and Bill dragged their canoe up onto the beach and began to walk away without a backward glance. I kept my eyes on the lake.

The first swimmer dove under the overturned canoe. Time seemed to go very slowly as I watched helplessly from the pier. Louise had reached the shore. She climbed up onto the pier, and someone handed her a towel. She stood next to me, shivering and watching silently as the lifeguard and the other swimmer kept diving in the area around the canoe.

Then the first diver came up, pulling Megan with him. Coughing and sputtering, she grabbed him around the neck in her panic. A voice, calm and clear, told her she was okay and he was going to swim her in to the shore. I recognized that voice. The swimmer who dove off the pier first was Austin!

He started toward shore, one arm around Megan, doing the sidestroke. I couldn't believe my eyes. He was swimming her in just the way we'd been learning in Junior Lifeguard class. The real lifeguard swam up to them and pulled Megan onto the paddleboard. Together they towed her in and came alongside the pier.

"I think you can stand up, Megan." Austin stood up to show her the water was at waist level. She tried to slide off the paddleboard and stand, but she was weak and unsteady. She was still coughing and her lips looked blue. The lifeguard slung an arm around her, and Austin supported her on the other side.

"Good job, Austin," said Kevin, as they walked Megan to the shore. She sat down on the sand where it met the pier. She was still shaking and coughing. Austin grabbed his towel and wrapped it around Megan's shoulders.

Jake and Bill were almost to the top of the hill. They hadn't even stayed to see if anyone would rescue Megan. She could have drowned out there. They had caused the accident, and it didn't even seem he cared.

"Parma! Carlson!" yelled Kevin. "Get down here!" He turned to me. "Brockway, there's a phone with my stuff on the tower. Would you get it, please?"

I returned with the phone and two dry towels. I put one around Megan's shoulders and handed the other to Austin. He rubbed it over his face. He was pale underneath his tan.

"That was great, Austin! You should try to get your Junior Lifeguard certification," I told him.

He looked up from drying his legs, then threw the towel around his shoulders. His eyes crinkled, and he sucked in his cheeks. He was trying not to laugh. Then I got it.

"You already have it!" I slapped my forehead in frustration. "You already have your freakin' Junior Lifeguard certificate." Of course he did. Once again, my younger brother had beaten me to a goal. Suddenly I felt very tired. "When did you get it?"

Austin folded the towel and handed it back to me. "Two years ago."

"You got Junior Lifeguard certification when you were ten?" I hadn't meant to screech. I just couldn't help it. The whole thing was so ridiculous. "Why didn't I know about this?"

Austin shrugged. "You didn't ask. You just assumed I was all brains and no brawn." He paused. "That means you thought I was intellectually superior but had no physical strength."

"I know what it means!" Actually, I didn't know what "brawn" meant, so I was glad he explained. I huffed out a long breath.

I turned back to Megan. She had huge goosebumps on her arms and her lips were tinged with blue. "Are you okay?" I asked her.

"Just cold. You probably think this whole thing was stupid. I mean, somebody my age should know how to swim."

The nurse ran down the steps, and she and the lifeguard replaced Megan's wet towels with a warm blanket. Then Miss Powell held Megan's arm as they started up the stairs. Austin, Jim, and I followed along behind.

"What happened to your life jacket, Megan?" I asked.

Megan glanced back at me over her shoulder. "I took it off. It was embarrassing being out there with that on."

"It's probably more embarrassing to drown," said Jim. He smiled at her.

"I know. It was dumb." Megan started to cough.

"You guys can talk later," said Miss Powell. "Megan needs to get checked over in the Emergency Room. We've called an ambulance." She called a Tracker girls' counselor to get Megan some dry clothes.

Kevin came up behind us and took Megan's other arm. "I can carry you, if you want," he said. Megan shook her head and trudged onward. It took them several more minutes to get up the stairs.

Jim and I walked back to our cabin to change.

I said, "I wonder what they'll do to Jake."

"They should send him home for this, don't you think?" said Jim.

I nodded. "Sounds like a plan to me."

Jake did not go home. The counselors did not discuss campers with other campers, so we didn't know what they might have reported. Apparently Jake told the camp director the incident was an accident. But Austin and I had watched Jake and Bill deliberately ram Megan's canoe. It was no accident.

That should have been enough drama for one day. But that night, I awoke to screams. I sat up fast, bumping my head on Jim's bunk. I reached for my flashlight. The other guys woke up too. Lights flashed back and forth in the darkness. Terry opened the screen door and came inside, followed by Levi.

"What's going on?" asked Terry.

Jake was standing next to his bunk, pointing at something long and black that was slithering under the covers. He was gasping for breath and didn't speak. His finger shook as he pointed.

"There," he gasped.

Levi drew close, eyeing the bunk. "What was it?"

"A snake," said Terry. "Not sure what kind. I didn't hear a rattle."

"Everybody get back out of the way," said Levi. "Go outside. We'll tell you when you can come back in."

Both counselors carried large flashlights. I watched through the screen as they directed the beams onto Jake's bed. Terry grabbed the covers and yanked them back. A long black snake with yellow stripes slithered toward them, burying itself under the blankets again.

"Garter snake," I said through the screen. "Not venomous."

Terry glanced at me through the screen door. "Yup. But fatal if it scares somebody to death."

Jake glowered at me. "You're the one who did it, aren't you. You put that damn snake in my bed. I'm going to...." He clenched his left fist and came at me. I put up an arm to block his punch. Levi flew out of the cabin and stepped between us.

"That's enough. You aren't going to do anything, Jake. How many times do I have to tell you about physical abuse of other campers?" He turned to the group of guys. "Did anyone see anything? Did you see anybody put a snake in Jake's bed?"

Everyone shook their heads, muttering that they hadn't.

"He did it!" shouted Jake, pointing at me.

"I didn't!" I yelled back. "I wouldn't do a mean thing like that to a snake."

"Why you..." Jake balled up his fist again.

Levi grabbed Jake's wrist. "If I see you do that again, I'll call your father to come and get you, tonight. Then I'll call the police and file a report. Got it?" He released Jake's wrist. Jake muttered something about calling his father himself. He never let anyone forget his dad was a lawyer.

"We have to catch this snake," said Terry. "Then you guys can go back to bed."

Levi went back into the cabin. "We need something to put it in."

"You could put it in a pillowcase," I said. "I think I can catch it."

"I'll help," said Jim.

We went back into the cabin, shutting the door quietly behind us. The snake had disappeared. I took the pillowcase from my pillow and opened it wide. "Chase it toward me, Jim."

Jim flattened himself over Jake's bunk and flapped the covers. The snake moved out from under the bunk. I gently covered it with the pillowcase and picked it up. "I'll let it go in the woods."

Jim and I took the snake outside to the trees. I set the pillowcase on the ground, partly open. The snake slid out and disappeared. It was probably glad to be back where it was safe.

When we got back to the cabin, everyone was inside, looking for snakes in their bedding. I didn't blame them. Whoever put the snake in Jake's bed might have done it to someone else as well. Jim and I checked our beds too, as everyone flipped back their covers, turned over their pillows, and peered under their bunks. Finally Jim climbed into his bunk, and I got into mine.

"I'm gonna get you for this, Brockway," muttered Jake.

"Right." I closed my eyes. It had been a very long day. A troubling thought kept me awake for a long time. Someone had put that snake in Jake's bunk. It wasn't me. So someone else had a reason to be angry at Jake Parma. Who was it?

Chapter Six—Shell Necklace

During free period the day after Megan almost drowned, I went to the Trading Post to get some ice cream. Austin was there, buying a purple rain poncho.

"Good color on you," I said.

"It's not for me." He handed the cashier some money.

"Who's it for?"

"None of your business." Austin put the bag under his arm and bought both of us a fudge bar. We followed the path to the Tracker woods and sat down on some logs to eat our treats.

"Why are you wearing long pants?" asked Austin. "It's ninety degrees out here."

I let out a long breath. Why was I keeping it from him? Was I ashamed of it? Yes, I was. Even though it wasn't my fault, I didn't want to admit to my brilliant, attractive, and talented little brother that the feathers were spreading. I had to tell somebody, though. Austin already knew they were under my arms, so he wouldn't be too surprised.

I reached down and pulled up my pant leg. Small white feathers covered my lower legs, extending all the way down to my ankles.

Austin stared at my leg, frowning. "Are they on both legs?"

"Yup. Arms too." I sucked on the fudge bar, but it was melting faster than I could eat it. Chocolate dripped onto my pants.

"We'll have to go home." Austin sounded alarmed. "You can't keep covering it up. What if it—"

"Don't say it." I didn't even want to think about having more feathers.

"But what if it does, Luke? You could wake up tomorrow morning with feathers on your face. They'll call an ambulance or something. Then we'll have a hard time getting out of here." He stood up. "Let's go. We'll call Gramps right now."

"How can we? Neither of us has a phone."

Austin grinned, showing all his teeth. "I have a phone. Mom gave it to me before we left. She knew I wouldn't use it unless there was an emergency." He put his arm around my shoulders, stretching up to do it. "This is an emergency, bro." He threw the last of his fudge bar into a trash can.

"What about the Fish Island campout?" I asked. "It's the day after tomorrow. Cooking over a campfire and sleeping under the stars are the things I like best about camp. We couldn't go to Fish Island last year because the weather was bad, so I don't want to miss it." I knew he'd been looking forward to it too.

"Plus I need the overnight to complete requirements for my camping badge." This wasn't a scout camp, but the counselors could sign off on badge skills.

"And I'll be fifteen in September, Austin," I reminded him, "This is the last year of camp for me, so it's my last chance. Besides, we won't be swimming," I added. "We'll be wearing jeans and long-sleeved shirts."

Austin made circles in the dirt with the toe of his shoe. "What about the feathers? If you get them on your face, what will you do?"

"You'll be there. I'll tell you if I get any prickly feelings on my face. We can take a boat back to camp. I'll be okay."

Austin rolled his eyes. "Right. How do you know?"

"I've discovered something important. When I do something that uses an eagle trait, such as eagle vision, it makes the feathers grow. Strong emotion such as anger makes them grow too."

"I'll keep an eye on you," said Austin. "I'll be able to see your face and you won't. So if I say it's time to go, we go. Agreed?"

"Agreed."

Austin was still holding the bag with the purple poncho.

"That's for Megan, right?" I nodded at the bag. "Is she your girlfriend?"

"Not my girlfriend. Just a friend. You're the one she likes."

I twisted to stare at him. Heat burned in my cheeks. Not this again. First Louise, and now Austin. He had to be kidding. I'd never thought of Megan that way. "How do you know?" I asked. "Did she say something?"

"Not exactly."

"Then how do you know?"

"From the way she looks at you."

"Please. You're the one she talks to. Why do you think she likes me?"

"Because she always finds a reason to be around you. She hangs around the mess hall after her group leaves so she can say hi to you. She does it every day." Austin took two wet wipes from his pocket. He handed one to me. "Haven't you noticed that?"

"No." That was a lie. I had noticed. Sometimes it embarrassed me, and other times it felt like she was just being friendly.

I wiped the chocolate from my mouth and hands and threw the wipe in the trash.

"Then there was the incident at the water fountain." Austin was relentless. He lifted his eyebrows, waiting.

I squinted at him, trying to remember. "What happened at the water fountain?"

"You turned the water on so she could get a drink," said Austin. "I saw you."

I scratched the back of my neck. "So what? I was just being polite, like Dad taught us. Holding doors. Stuff like that."

"Uh huh." Austin pushed himself up from the bench. "You touched her hair. I saw you." His tone of voice dripped with disapproval.

"It was falling into the fountain and getting wet. What was I supposed to do? Her arms were full of books."

"Seemed more than just a friendly touch to me."

I shook my head. Austin was being ridiculous. "Megan might like me as a friend. That's all. She's too young, Austin. She's your age."

I was going to high school in the fall. Ninth grade. Austin and Megan would both still be in middle school. Megan had been a good friend to me. She'd even saved my life. But no matter how much I liked her as a friend, I didn't want a girlfriend.

From what I'd heard, once girls became "girlfriends" things started getting complicated. They started asking why you hadn't called lately, when you'd just talked to them the day before. They got mad if you talked to another girl, even if it was about a lab assignment. They expected you to remember their birthdays and send them gifts on holidays. Who needed that? Not me. I had enough trouble remembering Mom's birthday.

Austin took a pack of gum from his pocket and offered me a stick. "Don't you like Megan?"

I sighed. Did we have to keep talking about this? "Sure" I said, unwrapping the gum. "I like Megan. She's nice. She's kind of cute, too. But I'm not looking for a girlfriend."

"It happens when it happens," said Austin.

"Austin, the love guru, speaks." I poked his arm. "I'll tell you what, buddy. It's not happening to me. I have things to do." It was time to end this conversation. I glanced at my watch. Free period was almost over.

"Someone is coming," said Austin. "Someone with red hair. You're already here, so it must be Megan."

At that moment, Megan hurried down the path. "I'm glad I caught up with you guys." She sounded breathless, as though she'd been running. "I wanted a chance to talk to you alone."

Austin raised and lowered his eyebrows twice. One corner of his mouth went up in a kind of sneering half-smile. What was going on here? He was the one who bought her a purple poncho.

"What do you want to talk to us about, Megan?" I asked.

She crossed her arms. "I want to discuss what happened to us at the zoo. I think I have a right to know, and Uncle Roy won't tell me anything." Her tone was defiant, like, "Tell me or else."

Austin scooted over to make room for her on his log. She sat down next to him and took a deep breath.

"Okay. I knew your family was cursed, and that was why you guys changed into animals," she said. "But Uncle Roy and I aren't in your family. So why did we change into animals during that storm?"

I glanced at Austin. His eyes met mine, and he shook his head slightly. We were thinking the same thing. In order for Megan and Mr. Gifford to be changed into animals, they had to be related to either Dunn Nikowski or Gramps. They weren't related to Gramps. That left Dunn Nikowski. Megan wasn't going to like hearing she was related to Dunn.

A cool breeze made the leaves flutter around us. Megan shivered. Austin opened his bag and put the purple poncho around Megan's shoulders.

"Thanks, Austin. What's the occasion?" She smiled at him, pulling the folds of the poncho closer. She was wearing the shell necklace. It was glowing, as though there was a flashlight behind the shell.

"It's an early birthday gift," said Austin. He pointed to the necklace. "Gramps told us about a necklace like this. You've heard the story, right?"

Megan shook her head. "No, I haven't."

"When Dunn was bitten by the Komodo, a medicine woman put a necklace like this one around his neck," said Austin. "It was supposed to help Dunn heal so he and Gramps could find another pink Komodo. She said they would also have the strength of three animals to help them. But if Gramps and Dunn didn't find a pink Komodo and return it to the people, the blessing would become a curse. They and their descendants could become animals for the rest of their lives."

"According to Gramps, the necklace was made of beads," I added. "It had a shell pendant, painted with a picture of a pink Komodo."

Megan swallowed. "Just like this one." She pointed to the pink Komodo on the shell.

I licked my lips. "Here's the thing, Megan. That might be the very same necklace."

Megan stared at the ground, her expression troubled. Then she looked up at me. "But all that was years and years ago."

"You said your grandmother sent it to you," I said. "Could you ask her where she got it?"

"I can't. I don't know how to find her."

I sat down on the log next to her. "After Gramps left on his ship, Dunn stayed on the island for a long time. He must have known your grandmother. I think he must have given her the necklace."

Megan's eyes were wide. "You think Dunn Nikowski gave my grandmother this necklace?"

"There's only one way to find out," said Austin. "You could ask her. Do you think she's still alive?"

Megan picked up a twig and began breaking little pieces of it. "Yes, she's still alive. She lives far away, on an island somewhere. I don't even know where it is."

"May I see the necklace?" I asked.

Megan lifted the necklace around her hair and handed it to me.

When the necklace touched my hand, I felt something strange. A kind of buzz flowed from it, as though the necklace could hum—as if power were flowing from the necklace into my hand and up my arm. The shell still glowed and now began to blink on and off. I moved the necklace to my other hand and the same thing happened. It felt like those little toys that zap when you touch them. I handed it back to Megan, glad to be rid of it.

"It just started to glow this week, said Megan. "But I've never seen it blink like that. Were you doing anything to it, Luke?"

"No. It just did that on its own." This was becoming a real mystery.

Austin held out his hand, and Megan placed the necklace on his palm. He frowned. The shell wasn't glowing the way it had when I held it. Austin felt something, though. I could tell by the look on his face that something happened when he touched it.

"What did you feel?" I asked.

Austin's brow wrinkled. I could almost see his brain cells hopping to attention. He closed his eyes. He sat still for so long I wondered if he'd gone to sleep.

Megan reached over and touched his hand. "Austin? Are you awake?"

His eyelids flickered. He opened his eyes and sighed. "Yes. I was listening for clues, trying to follow the shell's emanations."

"It's what? Speak English, Austin," I said. "You're getting more like Gramps every day."

"Thank you." Austin reached for his water bottle and took a drink. "I think I know why this thing reacts to Luke. It's meant to glow like that when it's near a Komodo dragon."

"Explain, please," said Megan.

"Did you ever play that game where you hide something and the person who hid it says that you're getting 'warmer' when you're getting nearer to the hidden item and 'colder' when you move away from it?"

He stood up, holding the necklace in front of him, and walked away from us. The pink light faded. Then he turned around and walked closer to me. The shell began to glow pink again. When I took it in my hand, it began to blink on and off.

"See what I mean?" said Austin. "It knows Luke has been a Komodo. That's why you just noticed the necklace glowing this week, Megan. It's because you've been wearing it when Luke is near."

Megan held her hand out and Austin gave her the necklace. The light stopped blinking.

"I think it will help us find a Komodo," he said. "I also think it can help us find a pink one, though I'm not sure how."

"Take good care of that necklace, Megan," I told her. "We may need it to find that special Komodo. Once we find it, we can break the curse. We'll be able to go to school and get good jobs. You're holding our future in your hands."

"Put it under your pillow at night," said Austin. "Don't leave it in your suitcase or backpack."

Megan pushed herself up from the log. "I still don't understand why the curse affected Uncle Roy and me."

"Do you have any other grandparents?" I asked.

Megan nodded. "I had another grandmother, named Helen. She and my grandfather were divorced when my mother and Uncle Roy were babies. He never came to see them, so they didn't know their father at all. And of course I never met him. He's probably dead and buried by now." She walked a little way from us and stood looking into the woods. Her expression was sad.

I glanced at Austin and found him looking at me. We were thinking the same thing. Megan was right. Her grandfather was Dunn Nikowski. Dunn was dead. We'd seen him die in the zoo parking lot. Our grandfather had killed him during their last battle.

"She doesn't get it," whispered Austin. "We have to say it clearly. We have to say 'Dunn Nikowski is your grandfather.'"

"I think she understands," I whispered. "That's why she's upset. Maybe we should talk about something else." I walked to the edge of the woods, where Megan was standing. I glanced at my watch. It was almost two PM.

"Don't you have archery class at two o'clock?" I asked.

Megan blinked. "Oh, my gosh! I'm going to be late." She started trotting back toward the baseball diamond and the archery range. Austin and I followed her.

"I don't know why I'm hurrying," said Megan. "My arm still hurts, so I can't pull the bowstring. I should have signed up for swimming lessons instead."

I jogged ahead so I could walk next to her. "You don't have to take swimming lessons, Megan. I've thought of a way you can learn how to swim. Fast."

Megan agreed to meet Austin and me down on the beach while everyone else was at supper. She waved goodbye and headed toward the archery range.

We'd given her the facts. She had changed into an animal, and only descendants of Gramps and Dunn Nikowski could do that. Dunn had provoked a rare pink Komodo. It bit off his leg, and Gramps had to shoot it. A medicine woman put a shell necklace around Dunn's neck while he was ill. Megan was wearing that necklace now. Her grandmother, who lived on an island far away, had sent that necklace to her. We didn't know who her grandmother was, but we knew the identity of her grandfather. Megan was a smart girl. She knew what we were trying to tell her. She had a hard truth to face and she wasn't ready. Yet.

Chapter Seven—Swimming Lessons

The three of us met that evening on the beach. It was the supper hour so everyone else was busy. Megan and Austin were in swimsuits. They walked into the water until they were about chest deep. I sat on the pier to watch.

"Megan, have you changed into any other animals besides the death adder?" asked Austin.

Megan shivered slightly. "No. I was afraid to try."

"You have two changes left, then. If you turn into an animal that swims, you can learn how at the same time. It will be fun."

"What kind of an animal?" asked Megan.

"A frog, maybe," said Austin. "Or a turtle."

"Or an otter," I added.

"An otter would be fun," said Austin. "I wish I had a change left."

"Maybe you do," I said. "I think we were wrong about that. I think it's the number of animals you change into, not the number of times you change."

Austin frowned at me. "Um, I have to think about that."

I knew why he was frowning. I'd only turned into three animals at the zoo; a Komodo dragon, a hippo, and an eagle. I still had animal traits from both the Komodo and the eagle. I nodded to Austin. "We'll figure that out later. Meanwhile, Megan has to decide what kind of swimming animal she'd like to try."

"It should be something that's common around here," said Austin. "That way no one will notice you when you're practicing."

Megan closed her eyes. "Let me see. I guess I'll be a frog. They're good swimmers. How do I change? We aren't having a geomagnetic storm. Or even an ordinary storm."

"We don't need one because we've changed into animals before," said Austin. "Just close your eyes and focus. Then get down under the water and picture yourself as a frog."

Megan took a deep breath and sank into the water, letting her head go under. Austin stood in the water near her. Seconds went by. Then a minute. It was very quiet.

"Can you see her?" I called out. "Is she okay?" Austin gave me a "thumbs up" signal.

More seconds ticked by. After another minute I saw circles forming on the top of the water. The water churned and bubbled, swirling as if a giant hand had reached down and pulled the plug on the lake. The bubbling stopped, and the water turned green and cloudy.

"Uh oh," said Austin. He hurried in to shore and waved for me to come with him. We ran toward the steps at the base of the hill together. "I was afraid of this," said Austin. He was panting as he pointed back to the lake.

"What?" I cried. "What's wrong?'

87

Up through the murky water rose two bulging eyes, about eight feet apart, on the sides of a curved mass of green skin. The skin stretched out to form a flat nose, covered with dark spots. A wide mouth stretched beyond the eyes on both sides. Beneath the mouth, a pulsing yellow throat blended into the fat, green body of an enormous frog. It was bigger than a Volkswagen Bug. It kept growing, stretching across the sand and expanding upwards until it was about the same size as my bedroom. I swallowed hard. This couldn't be Megan. Something must have happened to her. The wide mouth opened and a pinkish yellow tongue unrolled, snapping up a passing bluegill.

"Grummpke. Grummpke." The sound spilled from the frog's mouth like a low roar. A bullfrog. Aggressive as a bull protecting a herd, it hopped toward us, propelling itself into the air with a mighty thrust of its back legs. It landed a few yards away from us with an earth-shaking crash. On one side of the pier, rowboats slammed into one another, forced sideways by giant waves.

Austin and I ran up the steps and stared at the creature from behind the tag board.

"Are you sure that's Megan?" I whispered

"Megan," Austin called out, his voice clear and calm. "I think this experiment has gone a little too far."

"That frog is enormous." I kept my voice low. "Would Megan have had the concentration to do that?"

As if it heard me, the bullfrog let out another bellowing sound. *"Grummpke!"* It moved one front leg forward, churning up the sand and throwing some of it on me. If it decided to jump again, we'd be flattened.

Austin didn't seem worried. He stroked his chin, like he always did when he was thinking. "She's really amazing. She turned our little swimming idea into that huge creature. We didn't even talk about how to grow bigger." He stared at the giant frog, his face shining with admiration. "Imagine what she'll be able to do when she goes to college, Luke. What will she do with all that talent?"

All that talent was making me very nervous. "Right now I just hope she remembers that she could squash us like bugs," I said. "Or eat us like bugs," I added with a shudder. "Isn't she supposed to be learning to swim?"

Austin leaned back against a nearby tree. He didn't seem to be listening to me. "I don't think it's that hard to grow into a really huge animal. Remember Gramps and Dunn—how gigantic they grew during the fight in the zoo parking lot?"

"How did they do it?" I rasped, my throat suddenly dry. "We have to figure it out before we're frog food."

"She's not going to eat us." He walked back and forth, stroking his chin and nodding. If his hair was white he'd be a perfect miniature of Gramps.

The frog watched him as he walked, the tractor-tire-sized eyes swiveling right, then left then right again as Austin walked back and forth in front of her.

"Here's what you do," said Austin. "Focus on an image of the animal that's the size you want to be. Large or small."

I glanced nervously at the gigantic frog, then turned my attention to Austin. "Okay. Let's see you do it."

Austin set his water bottle on a nearby stump, then spread his feet apart, one slightly forward. He closed his eyes. He looked so calm and quiet I wasn't sure anything was going to happen. Then, right before my eyes, he started to grow. His body grew taller and heavier, covered with a new layer of muscle. His head grew bigger and began to look like a bear, with a long snout and short rounded ears. His neck thickened and slanted into massive shoulders. Broad, flat paws replaced his hands and feet. He reached a height of ten feet. He kept growing until he reached twenty feet. My brother the bear was now two stories tall.

"Stop!" I yelled. "That's enough."

The bear stood quietly for a minute or so. Then it began to shrink. I glanced around, expecting to see campers and counselors screaming and running at us, but the beach was quiet. No one was tearing down the hill. Everyone was still in the mess hall, busy with dinner. I waited nervously for the bear to fade away and my brother to return. It didn't take long. A few seconds later, Austin was back and in his human body.

"High five," he called out to the frog. The frog held out its right digits and Austin reached up and slapped it carefully.

He sat down on the ground. "I'm beat. That took a lot of energy." He glanced at the frog. "Apparently I didn't scare her."

"No. It seems to like us." I sat down next to him. The frog scooted forward as if it was trying to listen. "I wonder if I could do it. Get that big, I mean."

"You probably could, but I don't think you should try," said Austin. "You've already got feathers from becoming an eagle. We don't know what getting larger or smaller would do to you."

I nodded. As usual, Austin was right. If I experimented with changing size, I could end up looking like a Smurf.

He stood up. "Come on, Megan. You're supposed to be learning how to swim."

"Grummpke!" The frog jumped again, scattering sand and making the earth tremble. It hopped into the water, creating huge circles as it disappeared under the waves. A minute later, Megan surfaced. "Help!" she cried, waving her arms in the air. Austin took a floatation ring from the post and threw it into the water. "Thanks," yelled Megan. She kicked her way in to shore, pushing the ring ahead of her. When she stood up, I handed her a towel.

Austin cleared his throat. "Good job, Megan. Maybe next time, go a little smaller. That way you won't be so obvious. In case you don't want to be seen," he added. "And it will be easier for you to swim."

Megan grinned. "Pretty good though, don't you think? I hated being a tiny snake."

"I feel like someone is watching us," I said in a low voice.

Austin glanced toward the top of the long staircase. "Good call. Someone in a blue jacket just ducked behind a tree at the top of the hill. Jake was wearing a blue jacket earlier this afternoon."

"Don't worry about him," said Megan. "He'll keep his mouth shut. Or else."

"Or else what?" I asked. Jake hadn't kept his mouth shut about my feathers. Why would he keep silent about a bullfrog the size of a one-car garage?

Megan laughed. "I know a few things about him that he wouldn't want revealed."

"Let's try again, Megan," said Austin. "This time, keep the size down to a regular bullfrog. You need to do some actual swimming."

Megan lowered herself into the water and disappeared. I couldn't even see her from where I sat, but Austin was watching her closely. He walked around in the space enclosed by the sides of the pier, staying close in case she should need him. A large snapper or a big fish might want to eat her. After about fifteen minutes, Megan reappeared in human form.

"Okay," said Austin. "Time to see if our experiment worked. Hold onto this float board and kick like a frog. I'll demonstrate first." He took the board and showed Megan how to do the frog kick.

Megan took the board and followed Austin's directions. After a few tries she was doing the frog kick correctly. Then Austin showed her the arm stroke and how to combine it with the frog kick. Megan swam around him, propelling herself forward with the arm stroke and frog kicks.

I glanced at my watch. "We should get back upstairs before someone comes looking for us." Austin and Megan got out of the water. "Good job, both of you!" I handed them each a towel.

"You did really well, Megan," said Austin. "I think you'll be able to swim now."

"It makes me feel safer, anyway. Thanks for your help, Austin." They gave each other a "high five" hand slap again. Then we began the long walk up the wooden stairs.

"What made you change into that monster frog, Megan?" I asked.

"I was tired of not being noticed," said Megan.

"Not being noticed? I'm not sure what you mean." It seemed to me that everybody noticed Megan.

"Was I in the dining room today at lunch?" She stopped on the stair and turned around. Even though I was two steps lower, we were nose to nose.

I frowned, uncertain whether Megan was at lunch or not. "Ummm, I don't know."

"Exactly." She pivoted and continued climbing the stairs, gaining speed.

"What was that all about?" I asked.

Austin rolled his eyes to answer me. "The answer to the question she just asked you is 'yes.' She was at lunch. She went to your table to ask you something."

"I don't remember that." I frowned, thinking back to lunch period. "I wonder what she asked me."

"I'm guessing here, but she and her friends were talking about the dance Saturday night. She might have asked you if you were going."

"Really? I don't remember."

"And that would be the problem," said my brother, the love guru. "When she said she was tired of not being noticed, she was talking about you."

He ran up the stairs, taking them two at a time, until he caught up with Megan. I was several steps behind, but their voices carried in the quiet night.

"You don't have to turn into a thousand-pound bullfrog to get somebody to notice you," he told her.

She laughed. "Don't I?"

"I notice you anytime you're near. Lots of times when you aren't near." His voice was sad. I stood still for a moment to let them get further ahead of me on the stairs. I didn't want them to know I'd heard.

Megan reached out her hand. Austin took her hand in his, and they walked the rest of the way up the long stairway together.

Suddenly I felt empty, as if I'd just lost something I didn't know I wanted.

Chapter Eight—Pig Toss

Time was running out. Austin and I agreed to stay for the Fish Island campout, but after that we had to leave. We'd have to miss the second roping clinic, but at least we'd learned the basics. We could keep practicing at home.

Before we left, we needed to talk to Megan again. We had to make sure she understood that Dunn was her grandfather, and the shell necklace was the same one the medicine woman had given Dunn fifty years ago. We needed Megan's help. If we went back to Komodo Island, we'd need the shell necklace.

During free period the next day, Austin and I waited for her in in the same place we'd met before. There were trees all around us, and we couldn't be seen from the camp or the road.

"Megan is a smart girl," said Austin. "After everything we've told her, she must know she's related to Dunn."

"Knowing it and admitting it are two different things." I felt nervous and my mouth was dry.

"Here she comes," whispered Austin.

Megan came into the clearing. Austin patted the space next to him on a fallen tree and she sat down. "What's going on?" She looked from one of us to the other.

I took a drink of my water. "Megan, we have to ask you something. It's very important. It's the only way we can find out why you and your uncle were affected by this curse."

Megan huffed out a long breath, and her shoulders slumped. "I have a feeling I don't want to hear this."

"We told you about the curse that the medicine woman put on Gramps and Dunn Nikowski," said Austin. "All their descendants would be cursed too, until one of them found a pink Komodo and returned it to the village.

"We know you aren't related to Gramps." I added. "So somewhere in your family tree, you have to be related to Dunn. Are there any other relatives you could ask?"

"I have an aunt. And a cousin." She wrinkled her nose as if something smelled bad. "My cousin is a pig."

Austin grinned. "Sounds like you don't like him much."

Megan shrugged. "I don't like him at all. It would be nice if we got along, because he's the only cousin I have. His parents are divorced and his father has custody. His mother, my Aunt Jo, is Uncle Roy's sister. I met her once, long ago. She lives in another country now. I have no other relatives I can talk to, except Uncle Roy."

"You have us," said Austin. "We went through all that stuff at the zoo together. We're really the only ones who know about that."

"Actually, there's someone else who knows," said Megan. "You'll be meeting him any second now. I asked him to join us."

She pointed towards the woods where some bushes were rustling. A rhythmic pounding started, like a horse's hooves clomping hard dirt. I could feel the vibration in the ground under my feet. Chills ran up my spine. Something was coming. Something heavy.

Seconds later, a huge, dark shape thundered through the tree line. It was an animal of some kind, at least three feet high and maybe four feet long. It weighed about three hundred pounds, maybe more. Sharp tusks projected from each side of a snout that looked half pig and half wolf. The beast slid to a stop at the edge of the clearing, tossing its head and staring at each of us in turn. I knew what it was, though I'd never seen one before. It was a wild boar, a mutation of nature. Wild pig. Feral swine. Whatever it was called, this monster had nothing to do with those nice pigs that farmers raised. This pig was furry, oversized and swollen with meanness. It lowered its head, tusks aimed for my groin. Austin stepped out in front of us, arms apart as if ready to do battle.

"You can't catch him," cried Megan, pushing herself ahead of him. "He'll run you down!"

For a moment I froze, as if time had suddenly stopped. Then, in the next three seconds, several things happened at once. I grabbed Megan and swung her out of the way. Austin and I moved in front of her, our bodies blocking her from the boar's sight. I felt Austin quiver next to me, and immediately felt safer. He could explode into grizzly form in nanoseconds if he wanted. He was waiting, controlling the impulse to morph. Beneath my skin, I could feel the prickling of scales. Sharp nails stabbed the insides of my fingers and toes, ready to turn them into claws. I took a deep breath and held back. I would change forms only if it was necessary. No way could this big bad piggy take us both.

The beast put its head down and scraped its right hoof like a bull getting ready to charge. The massive head moved slightly, changing its focus. Now it was aiming those sharp, pointed tusks directly at Austin. It pawed the ground, snorting and grunting as if it were towing an RV. Then he thundered forward.

Megan tried to shove Austin out of the path of the pig. My brother didn't move.

"Stay out of the way, Megan," I shouted. "You'll get hurt."

Megan ignored me. She slid sideways between us and yelled at the top of her voice, "Knock it off, or else!"

The pig skidded to a stop in front of us, spraying twigs, leaves, and dirt into our faces. Close up, I could see how big it really was. This was the biggest, ugliest pig I'd ever seen. It was far bigger than those blue ribbon pigs they show at county fairs, the ones that stretch across the whole pen. Those pigs could win beauty contests compared to this one. Its snout was longer than a wolf's muzzle, flattened at the end by wide piggy nostrils. Those two long, sharp tusks could pulverize anything they skewered, especially at ramming speed.

Austin and I stared at the pig. I turned to Megan. "That pig could have killed you. How did you get it to stop?"

She shrugged. "He doesn't want to get bitten by the death adder. He knows I'll do it, too."

The pig trotted in a circle, then backed up. It turned to face us.

My throat was so dry I couldn't speak. My pulse pounded in my ears. I was quivering, prickling on the edge of change. Austin still didn't move. He stood silent as a statue, but I knew he was sizing up the situation, planning both defense and offense. Around us, the forest was strangely quiet, as though insects, birds, and woodland creatures had evacuated the area. The only sounds were my ragged breathing and the pig's sloppy snorts.

"He's one of us," Austin said at last. "It's Jake."

"It's Jake?" I stared at Megan. "Jake is your cousin?" That meant Jake was related to Dunn Nikowski too. Somehow, that didn't surprise me.

"Afraid so." Megan sighed. "He's a pig. A big, fat, mean pig. And that's when he's human. I almost like him better this way."

Austin nodded at me. "I think we should teach this pig a lesson. He's been asking for it since we got here."

The wild boar dug his left hoof into the dirt, lowering his massive head once more. Then it spoke, its words coming out in gravely bursts. "You first, baby bear. Then I'll eat the bird."

The bird? Nope. Not this time. My body was covered with purple bruises from Jake's viselike pinches. It was time for payback, but not from an eagle. The payback would come from something bigger and far more dangerous.

Austin roared, stretching to a height of ten feet, his arms and torso growing in length and girth. Fur bloomed over his tanned skin, sprouting until his body was covered with a thick brown pelt. His face turned into the wide, furry mug of a grizzly bear, ears rounded near the top of his head. His muzzle extended, opening to show a set of sharp white teeth. Incisors three inches long snapped together as he closed his mouth on a roar. I was glad he wasn't coming after me.

"Stand back," I whispered to Megan.

"Should I bite Jake?" she whispered. "I can morph into the death adder."

"Not this time. Save it for when we really need it." Megan nodded and hid behind a tree. I threw my body to the ground.

The Jake-boar squealed. "That's right, pukey Lukey. Get your head down and out of the way."

He was bluffing, backing away from Austin. He wasn't getting away. Not this time.

The Jake-boar faced my brother, so he didn't notice the nails piercing through the ends of my fingers and toes. The muscles in the back of my throat clenched, and venom pooled in my mouth. I could swallow that boar in three or four bites. No. No, I couldn't. I was a human in a Komodo form, not the other way around. I wanted to teach Jake a lesson, not eat him. In fact, the thought turned my stomach.

The boar snarled again, then charged, running hard at Austin's furry legs. Wrong decision. He should have run the other way. He should have run back into the forest and kept on going. The Austin-bear had grown to a height of fifteen feet. He stepped casually aside, and the charging boar raced past him, smacking into a tree trunk with its tusks. The tree groaned as the pig yanked its tusks out of the wood. The gigantic pig wheeled around, scraping its hooves against the ground. It charged again. Austin was still growing. He was now twenty feet tall. He bent and caught the wild pig by the legs, just above its flailing hooves. Turning in a circle, he swung the squirming swine around his body. He twirled, raising and lowering the pig as he turned. The pig hit the ground and bounced. Then Austin swung him up into the air again, slamming him into a low branch. Finally he held the Jake-pig by its front legs, the snout and piggy eyes facing him.

"You gonna behave now?" growled Austin. The pig swore, saying some nasty words. Mom would have washed his mouth out with soap. "Guess not," said Austin. "Let's play ball."

"Good," squealed the Jake-swine. "I'll break that bird boy's neck."

Austin twirled again, swung the pig over his head, and let him fly. Megan looked up, watching her cousin tumble over a nearby tree. He was going to land near me.

Power rushed into my limbs, inflating my body with iron strength. The intense force pushed my body to double its size, covering me with an armor of tough, bristling scales. I pushed myself up on four strong, bowed legs and pounded the earth with my tail. Twigs and fallen branches launched into the air, scattering behind me. When the pig landed, I pounced. Ten feet and three hundred pounds of deadly Komodo dragon, I flattened myself across his flabby pig belly. I flicked my forked tongue, poisonous saliva bursting from my mouth.

"You...you..." the boar stuttered, his piggy eyes bulging. "You're supposed to be an eagle."

"Is that so?" I flicked my forked tongue again.

My mouth watered. Holding the pig down with my upper body, I opened my jaws wide and showed all my teeth. The muscles in the back of my throat gulped, acting on some ancient reptilian instinct.

"Don't eat him yet." The Austin-bear's voice was calm. He glanced at his claws, turning them back and forth, admiring them as if he'd just had his nails done. "Let's play ball first.

We can eat him later. I do love a good pork barbeque. Honey barbeque sauce with a few pickles."

The pig squealed, shoving at me with all four hooves.

"One bite is all it will take to inject venom and thin the blood," I said calmly. I fixed the pig with a reptilian glare. "Komodo bites bleed a lot, causing the prey to become weak. You know that, right? Then the animal can't get away. There's nothing as frustrating as having your dinner get up and leave the table when you're ready to eat."

The pig swallowed a shout, gargling his words.

"What was that?" I asked politely, flicking my forked tongue. I didn't wait for an answer. I rolled the Jake-pig over and over, bumping him along with my head to the place where Austin stood. The sound of giggling came from behind the nearest tree. Austin scooped up the Jake-boar and dangled him by his feet.

"You had enough?" growled the Austin-bear.

The pig snuffled and gasped some words that sounded like, "I give."

I waddled over and flicked my forked tongue at him. "No more pinching," I hissed.

Austin gave him a couple of shakes. "No more bullying or insults. No more teasing, tormenting, or touching anybody. You or any of your friends do anything at all—step one toe out of line—and we'll be back." He dropped the pig with a thud.

Jake lay in the dirt, breathing hard as the pig form dissolved from his body. He rolled over and pushed himself up from the ground. He moved slowly, tiredly, as though he'd been in a ten-hour battle. He bent over, hands on his knees, still gasping for breath. I swiveled my gaze sideways at Austin. He stood still, arms crossed, watching Jake.

Jake straightened to his full height and pushed the hair out of his eyes. "Two against one."

"It was four against one when you and your buddies tackled Luke," said Austin. "This isn't the end of it. You pull anything again and we'll be back."

Jake squared his shoulders, jabbing a finger first at Austin and then at me. "That wasn't my only form. Next time, I'll be ready."

Austin shrugged. "Whatever. Just so you know, we have other forms, too. What you saw today was tame. So watch yourself."

Muttering to himself, Jake stalked away.

"And stay away from Megan," I yelled after him.

It took us longer than usual to morph back. The scales were fading from my body slower than a snail moves. We talked as we continued to regain our human bodies.

"Do you think we're enjoying this too much?" I asked.

Austin nodded. "Maybe. Remember that day at school when I knocked Jerry Magee into the janitor's supply cart?"

I laughed. "Yes. Toilet paper rolls shot into the air and rolled all over."

Austin took a deep breath. He wasn't smiling anymore. "I've never forgotten what you said to me that day. You said, 'If Magee had hit the wall, he could have broken his neck.' Magee could have been paralyzed for the rest of his life because of me."

"We could have hurt Jake badly, I guess," I said.

"While he was in the body of that monster wild pig?" Austin shook his head. "Probably not. But I don't think I want to do this again."

"Neither do I. Unless we have to defend ourselves or someone else," I added. "It was self-defense this time. At least it started that way."

We sat quietly for a moment. Austin was already back in his human form. Still part Komodo, I lay on the ground in front of him. I raised my hand, which was still covered with scales, and said, "For self-defense only."

Austin touched my claw with his hand. "For self-defense only."

My scales melted into my body one limb at a time. The claws retracted into my hands and feet, and my reptile head became human again. I hoped the feathers might go away, too. I checked my arms. They were still there, and more of them. Now the feathers extended almost to my wrist. The ones next to my skin were soft and white, but another layer of tougher feathers had sprung up behind them, some gray and some black. I let out a long breath. How was I going to cover these things up?

"Can I come out?" called Megan.

"Sure," said Austin. "He's gone."

Megan paused and stared at my arm. My sleeve was pushed up, and white feathers peeked out from under it. She reached over and gently touched one. Heat flushed into my cheeks. Quickly I pushed my shirt sleeve down over the feathers. "This is why we have to undo the curse, Megan. Or we're all going to end up looking like freaks."

"Does your grandfather know about this?" Megan's voice was soft.

I shook my head. "Not yet."

"I'm so sorry." Megan put her hand over mine.

"I've got a bad bruise," said Austin. "Don't I get any sympathy?" He held out an arm, where a spot the size of a baseball was slowly turning colors. Somehow Jake's fist had gotten through his fur.

"Let me see that," said Megan, walking over to him. "Maybe you should go see the nurse."

Austin pulled his arm out of her reach. "Never mind. It's fine." His cheeks were stained pink. His mouth was a tight, straight line across his face. I'd never seen him act that way before. Well, maybe once. Last fall he was reading over my shoulder. I swung my fist backwards, just to make him back off. Instead I hit him in the face and gave him a bloody nose. I made him cry.

Austin was tough. Physical injuries never made him cry. He had cried then because I hurt his feelings. That's what this was about. Megan had hurt his feelings by paying attention to me.

We didn't talk as we walked back to camp. We split up at the baseball diamond, going to our different camps. I waved to Austin. "See you later." He didn't answer. He stood with his back to me, looking in the direction that Megan was going. She was walking slowly, her head down as though she was watching the path for snakes. She did not look back.

I sighed as I watched them go. Austin liked Megan—a lot. Megan liked Austin, but she also liked me. I liked her back, but only as a friend. I wasn't looking for a girlfriend, but it looked like Austin was. This was worse than having feathers.

Chapter Nine—The Nightmare Begins

I cleaned up and got to the mess hall too late for supper, but Jim had saved me a plate. What a great friend—even if he had eaten half my dessert.

It was movie and popcorn night, so everyone cleared their tables and helped set up the chairs for the movie. It was one I'd already seen, so I helped fill the popcorn bags and hand them out, snacking as I went along.

Austin was in the popcorn line. He came up close and whispered to me. "Have you seen Megan anywhere?"

"Not since we split up after the battle." I handed him a heaping bag of popcorn. He'd missed dinner too.

"I just wondered if she was okay." My usually calm brother sounded worried.

"Isn't she here?" I scanned the room. Since the lights had been turned out for the movie, I couldn't see much, even with eagle-improved vision. "She's probably around somewhere. Maybe she went to the bathroom."

"Right." Austin went back to his group, but I could see him craning his neck to survey all the rows of chairs.

When the movie was over, we had milk and graham crackers, then went back to our cabins. I waited until everyone was through in the bathhouse, then took my turn. The other guys were already asleep in their beds by the time I got back. I slid under the covers and plumped the pillow under my head. I was tired, but something was nagging at me. I closed my eyes and took some deep breaths to relax. Soon I felt myself drifting into an exhausted sleep. Then I heard something strange.

Help me! Please help me. I'm going to die if no one comes to help me.

I opened my eyes. I'd heard those words clearly, but no one was awake. It must have been my imagination. I closed my eyes again. Turning on my side, I tried to go to sleep.

Help me. Someone, please help me or I'm going to die. He left me out here alone. Luke, can you hear me?

I sat up in bed, wide awake now. No one had spoken out loud, but I was sure I'd heard a cry for help. This time it called my name! I wasn't dreaming, was I? I crept quietly out of bed and put on my shoes and my jacket. Taking my flashlight and pocketknife, I eased through the screen door without making a sound. I didn't know what I was going to do with the knife, but I felt safer with it on me. I was scared. Really scared. Should I wake up one of the counselors? And tell him what? That I heard someone calling for help? We'd listen and hear nothing, then he'd tell me it was a dream and to go back to bed. No. If there was someone out there who needed help, I'd have to find him myself. Then I could tell the counselors.

The night Gramps, Austin, Mr. Gifford, and I escaped from the zoo, a big storm caused the power to go out. There was no power to the security fences, so many animals escaped from their enclosures and roamed the zoo. We hid in a building and found two wolves crouched there in a corner. Somehow I knew they were scared. I sent my thoughts to them, telling them what to do. They seemed to hear me. They followed my directions and went safely back to the wolf field. That was the first time I'd noticed an ability to communicate with animals.

Someone or something was trying to reach me in that same way now, through my thoughts. Maybe I could try to respond the same way—using my thoughts. I stopped in the darkness and focused, trying to listen. The voice was still there.

Luke, can you hear me? Please help me. I can't last much longer.

Where are you? I formed the question in my mind and concentrated on sending it. If I'd heard someone's thoughts, they'd better be listening for my answer. I sent the thought again. *Where are you?* Closing my eyes, I waited for a response.

Woods...across road. Tied. ... Hurry.

The words were weaker, but I heard the message clearly. Someone was in the woods across the road, tied. What did that mean? Was someone tied to a tree? It must be someone who couldn't shout or cry out. As soon as I was away from the cabins, I started to run. I ran until I reached the road, then hurried across. Stopping, I surveyed the trees. The voice came into my mind again.

I'm here. Can't you see me?

I looked around, but I couldn't see anyone tied to a tree.

Here, Luke. Walk further. Look down. The voice was very weak now. I could hardly hear it.

Watching the ground, I walked several more feet into the woods. I stopped short, nearly tripping over it in the dark. What I saw made my heart plummet. Who would do such a thing?

A huge snapping turtle was turned on its back, with all four legs tied to wooden stakes so it couldn't get away. It turned its head toward me, opening and closing its mouth as if it was trying to get air. I knelt beside it and took out my jack-knife.

"Were you trying to call me?" I asked. I hadn't heard any mental messages since I arrived. "I'm going to cut the ties. Don't be afraid."

Working gently, I slid the knife under the tie with the sharp side pointed up. As I freed each leg, the turtle tried to move it. When all four legs were free, the turtle stretched them out, flailing against the air. It was trying to turn over. It rocked first one way then the other, getting almost to the edge of its shell and then falling back again. The turtle was too weak to turn itself right side up.

"I'm going to turn you over," I said. "Please don't bite me." The turtle's head fell back against the ground, eyes closed. Was I too late? Was it dying? "Please don't die," I whispered. "I'm going to help you."

Gingerly, I picked up the big turtle and turned it over. It was heavy—heavier than a ten-pound bag of flour. There was a note taped to its shell. I pulled it off and read it.

No animal will make a fool out of me.

The words seemed familiar, as if I'd heard them somewhere before.

The turtle was breathing raggedly. How long had it been tied up like that? It must be hungry, or thirsty. I touched its front leg. The skin was dry and cold. Reptiles are cold-blooded and rely on their surroundings for warmth. It was a cool night. I took off my jacket and spread it over the turtle, then sat back on my heels to watch. I didn't know what else to do to help it.

After a few seconds the jacket began to move. It rose up from the ground a couple of inches, then flopped back down. The jacket's sleeves moved through the wet grass. I heard a sneeze. I'd never heard a turtle sneeze before. Two long legs kicked out from one side of the jacket. A mop of red hair emerged from the other side. Megan sat up. She sneezed again.

"It's....it's you!" I stuttered. "I didn't know you could change into a turtle!"

"Austin told me to try something smaller," said Megan. She put her arms through the sleeves of my jacket and pulled it on. She was shivering. "So I chose this form. I figured I would skip dinner and the movie to practice. I was swimming along nicely when Jake grabbed me with a big net."

"How did he know it was you?"

"I'm not sure he does," said Megan. "He could just be getting revenge against the turtle that bit him."

I nodded. "That might be. All turtles probably look alike to him."

"He's crazy," said Megan. "He could have killed me. He left me there to die."

"You said he might not know it was you."

"It doesn't make any difference. He was torturing a poor, helpless animal." Her eyes blazed with anger.

I didn't blame her. I was angry, too. "Why couldn't you change back?" I asked, helping her up. She was still wobbly.

"I panicked and tried to change back, but I couldn't. I couldn't concentrate because I was so scared."

We walked single file on the path that led back to the Tracker camp. When we reached the place where the path divided, we stopped. Megan took off my jacket and handed it to me. Her hair was damp and slicked down to her head. Her face was pale, and there were streaks of mud on her cheeks. She was still shivering.

"You'd better get back to your cabin and get warm. Won't your counselors be out looking for you?"

"I told them Uncle Roy was picking me up for a family funeral, and I'd be back late." She smiled at me. "Thanks, Luke. You saved my life. Again." She turned and ran for the Tracker cabins. I watched until she was out of sight, then headed back toward the Warrior camp.

I'd gone about twenty yards when Jim stepped out of the shadows. I rolled my eyes. "Are you going to follow me when I go back to school?"

"I didn't interfere, did I? I just wanted to make sure you were okay."

"How much did you see?"

Jim grinned. "I watched a big ugly snapping turtle turn into that cute redhead. So she's part of this too?"

"Unfortunately for her, yes." We were near the cabin now, and neither of us spoke again. We slipped noiselessly into the cabin and then into our beds. Once again I heard the crinkling of paper overhead. I poked the underside of the mattress over my head, and a few seconds later a small candy bar hit me in the face. "Thanks, buddy," I whispered into the darkness. I peeked at the wristwatch I'd shoved under my pillow.

It was almost midnight. I was so tired I could hardly move. Closing my eyes, I fell into an uneasy sleep.

My sleep was disturbed by nightmares. A giant Komodo was chasing me. I felt his hot breath and then the cold, scaly flesh. He knocked me down and pounced on me. I pushed him away with all my strength and sat up, my head bumping Jim's bunk. I rubbed the sore spot on my head, pushing the nightmare away.

The cabin was dark and quiet except for a couple of snores. I swung my legs off my bunk and sat there a minute, taking deep breaths and trying to slow my heartbeat. Taking my wristwatch out from under my pillow, I saw that it was now one o'clock in the morning. Everyone was tucked under their blankets except for one. Jake's bunk was empty. Where was he?

A beam of light danced across the screened windows. I ducked just in time. The light wandered to the other side of the cabin and then back toward me. I flattened myself on the bunk and closed my eyes. In a few seconds the light went off, and I heard the sound of footsteps moving away from the cabin. Maybe Jake was just going to the bathroom, but I didn't think so.

Sliding into my shoes, I picked up my flashlight and let myself out of the cabin for the second time that night. Jake was about thirty yards ahead of me. I could see his outline clearly. He wasn't heading toward the bathhouse. He was heading toward the front entrance of the camp. His head was down and he walked quickly, as though he had to get there in a hurry. I stayed well back, keeping him in sight. He had almost reached the road when I saw the headlights of a car flash onto the two stone pillars that marked the camp's entrance.

The car slid to a stop. I squatted behind some bushes and stayed still.

As Jake approached the car, someone rolled down the front driver's side window. I could hear the murmuring of voices. The person driving the car was male. He asked Jake if anyone had followed him.

"No," said Jake. He twisted back in my direction. He couldn't see me, since I was hidden by the hedge. The person in the car handed him a package about as big as two shoeboxes, then another the same size. I eased backwards so he wouldn't see me and bumped into two strong arms. I almost yelped, but in the next second I knew it was Jim.

"Let's get back to the cabin before he finds us gone," I whispered.

We crept back, Jim moving almost noiselessly in front of me.

"What do you think is in those packages?" he asked quietly.

"Don't know."

We didn't speak again. Jim soundlessly opened the cabin door. We tiptoed inside, climbed into our bunks, and pulled up the covers. None of the other guys had moved. Bill was snoring, and the others breathed evenly and quietly in their bunks.

It was almost ten minutes before Jake came back, empty-handed. He must have hidden the packages somewhere between the road and the cabin. What was in them? It had to be something he wasn't supposed to have at camp, or it wouldn't have been delivered at one in the morning by someone old enough to drive a car—and it was a nice car from what I could see, not a rusted heap.

Jake climbed into bed. I kept my eyes closed and my breathing regular. A few minutes later, Jake started to snore.

Opening my eyes, I stared at the patterned mattress bulging through the springs of the bunk above me. There was a tiny sound of paper ripping. Then came the smack of lips and an almost silent crunch. I poked the mattress. Jim's arm swung down from the upper bunk and tossed another small, wrapped candy bar onto my chest. I unwrapped it carefully so the paper wouldn't make any noise, then slid the chocolate into my mouth and let it melt. If there was chocolate in Jake's mysterious packages, he'd be the most popular guy at camp. If he shared it, that is, which he probably wouldn't.

As tired as I was, I couldn't get back to sleep. What was in those packages? Probably something illegal. Was it drugs? Alcohol? I hadn't heard any bottles clinking. What else would fit in two packages about the size of boot boxes? It was sure to be something that would cause problems, hurt somebody, or get our cabin in trouble. If I got to the packages first, I could turn them in to one of the counselors and say I found them. That would stop whatever trouble Jake planned to cause.

I rolled on my side and pretended to be asleep. Squinting into the darkness, I peered at the other bunks. Sounds of breathing, hushed and rhythmic, were broken by an occasional snort. Bill, in the bunk above Jake, muttered something and turned over. Bill talked in his sleep, so I wasn't worried. Jake was still snoring. He snorted once, then shifted so his back to me. He was still asleep. I slipped out of my bunk, picked up my shoes and my flashlight, and once again eased carefully outside.

Sitting on a log, I slipped on my shoes. A mosquito landed on my arm. I brushed it away, not wanting to make noise by slapping it. The cabin door open noiselessly and Jim came out, carrying his sneakers. We didn't speak. He handed me packet of mosquito repellent and bent to tie his shoes. We headed toward the road, walking so quietly we couldn't hear our own steps. It was hard to see. The tall trees blocked out most of the moonlight, and the dense brush hid the safety lights.

"How do you think we should do this?" I whispered, when we were about fifty yards away from the cabin. "There are a lot of places he could have hidden those packages."

"Not really." Jim spoke softly. "He was only a few minutes behind us. So he must have hidden them close to the path. Look in hollow logs, behind patches of brush, places like that."

"Okay. You take the left side and I'll take the right. Go in about ten yards. If we don't see anything, we can go further away from the path on the way back."

Jim nodded and crossed to the left. The circles of light from our flashlights skimmed the ground, then skipped in the brush and up onto the trees. The circles danced up and down, back and forth, growing larger, smaller, and then larger again as we searched for likely hiding places. Chipmunks scattered, chattering angrily at being awakened. Though we tried to be quiet, our footsteps sounded like clomping in the still, dark night.

A twig snapped somewhere ahead of us, followed by the tiniest sound of movement. Jim and I froze, listening. Another snap, and crunching underfoot. The noise was ahead of us. It seemed to be coming from an area about twenty yards away. My mouth went dry. Even the insects had gone quiet. Something was definitely out there. Or someone.

Jim picked up a stone and hurled it into the woods. Something dashed through the trees, scattering leaves and snapping twigs as it ran. A brown blur flew past us and disappeared in the direction of the bathhouse.

"A buck," whispered Jim. "Looked like a ten-pointer."

I'd noticed the antlers too, but my heart was pounding so hard I couldn't speak, let alone count the points. I nodded and focused my quivering circle of light back on the woods.

We left the path and checked out an area about twenty yards in diameter, about fifty yards from the mess hall.

"Here's a likely spot." Jim stopped, aiming his flashlight into a tree. In the tree's trunk, close to the ground, was a large opening about a foot high and two feet wide. He stepped back, moving the beam of his light away from the hole. "Could be an animal in there."

"Or a snake." I sniffed the air, then froze. "Smell that?"

Jim sniffed. "Yup. That's the odor of a big cat. Let's see if there are any tracks near the tree."

The beam of Jim's flashlight scoured the ground, then came to an abrupt halt. I went to his side and looked down. Tracks. Cat tracks. Very large cat tracks. The cougar was back!

"These tracks are fresh," whispered Jim. "It was probably stalking that deer. It could be watching us right now."

I shivered, remembering the cougar, large and tawny, padding silently along the tree limb over Megan's head three days ago.

I aimed my light up into the trees, checking nearby branches. Pushing aside leaves and twigs, Jim uncovered several more tracks. They led deeper into the woods, away from the path.

"I think it's headed away from the road," said Jim.

"These tracks are fresh," I whispered. "It's close. We should let somebody know."

Jim stood up, and we started down the path toward our camp.

"Don't run," said Jim. "If it's watching it might get the idea to chase us."

We walked as fast as we could, hurrying away from the woods and back toward our cabin. My heart was pounding. I could almost feel the stab of the big cat's claws as he landed on my back. I could protect myself if I had to. I could protect Jim, too. If I had to go Komodo, I would.

"They're going to ask what we were doing out here," I said, as we neared Terry and Levi's tent. "We might lose swim privileges or something."

Jim shrugged. "There's nothing else we can do." We were thinking the same thing. Even if we got into trouble, we had to tell the counselors the cougar was back. Everyone's safety was at stake.

Standing outside the tent, we could hear Levi and Terry snoring peacefully.

"Levi," I whispered. No one answered. I raised my voice a little. "Levi, Terry, wake up." Still no answer. Finally, I poked my head inside the tent and spoke in a low voice. "Terry? Levi? Sorry to wake you up."

Levi lifted his head and stared at me. "Luke? What's wrong?"

"The cougar is back. Jim and I just saw fresh tracks. I could smell it, so we know it's close by. The tracks are in front of a tree, about fifty yards from the mess hall."

Levi swung his legs over the edge of his cot, then reached over to shake Terry.

"What?" Terry's voice was grumpy.

"Luke and Jim found some fresh cougar tracks," said Levi. "Bring a light."

"Why didn't you tell us before we went to bed?" asked Terry. He fumbled in the crate he used as a dresser and found a lantern. He pushed back the flap and stepped out into the cool night air. Levi followed him, carrying his phone and a large flashlight.

"This way," I said, waving for them to follow.

We walked quietly for a few minutes until we came to the place where we'd seen the tracks. Jim found them again, brushing away more leaves. Levi flashed his light onto the tracks, then squatted to look more closely. Terry aimed his light into the trees on the far side of the road.

"The tracks look about the same size as the ones we saw a couple of days ago," said Levi. He stood up, brushing dirt from his hands.

"These tracks are fresh," said Jim. "That's why we woke you guys up."

"I guess we'll have to call the director," said Levi. "That cat could be anywhere."

"It's not far away," I said. "I can smell it."

Levi sniffed the air. "Smells like it's right around the corner."

"Or closer," said Jim.

I shuddered at the thought. "Let's go back to our camp to talk," I said. "We need to get away from this area."

"Mrs. Harris will probably want all the kids brought into the hall," said Terry, as we walked back toward Warrior camp. When we'd gone about a hundred yards, Terry stopped and turned around. He put his hands on his hips and stared at us as though the whole thing was our fault. "Everyone is going to hate being dragged out of bed in the middle of the night."

"What if we had all the counselors make a fire?" I suggested. "Then maybe you wouldn't have to get all the kids up."

"Some of the campfire pits are pretty far from the cabins," said Levi. "That might not be close enough to keep the cat away from them. The screen doors and windows aren't much protection, either." He punched some numbers into his phone and spoke into it, giving his name and the location of the tracks. He listened, glancing at us. "No, I don't know what the campers were doing out there this time of night. We'll talk to them tomorrow. Right now we need to know what you want done." He listened again, then put the phone back into the pocket of his sweatpants.

"To the hall with sleeping bags," he announced. "No exceptions. She's notifying the other counselors now."

"So she thinks that's safer than just letting the kids stay in their cabins?" said Terry.

"Cougars are shy. They aren't going to attack kids in a big noisy group," I explained.

"Mrs. Harris wants to know exactly where everyone is," said Levi. "If we left the kids in the cabins, they might get up during the night to go to the bathroom. Wandering alone out there, they'd be easy prey for a cat."

"So would counselors sleeping in tents," I added. "It was a good thing we found the tracks before the cougar found you guys."

Chapter Ten—Pandemonium

Beams of light waved and flickered from four different directions as kids trooped through the dark night, balancing rolled-up sleeping bags, shower bags, and flashlights in their arms. Nervous giggles, laughter tinny with sleep, and incoherent muttering blended with the loud chirp of crickets. The campers clustered in large groups, making as much noise as possible. Warriors section B, all three cabins, walked together. Levi strode in front of us and Terry behind, both of them directing beams of light from right to left, watching for any sign of the cougar. It wasn't going to come out of hiding with all these noisy kids around. But a lone camper, going out to the bathhouse, might not be so lucky.

We hadn't had time to check that big tree hole to see if Jake had stowed the packages there. When we saw those tracks, Jim and I took off. A mountain lion will attack humans, and the experts weren't sure what people should do if they met one. If you ran, the lion might chase you. If you stood still, it might kill you more easily. It was probably best to stay in a group and not walk around alone in a wooded area where they lived. But who knew for sure where they lived? They weren't supposed to live here, in Lower Michigan, but I'd seen one with my own eyes. And where there was one, there might be another.

I felt a lot safer when we arrived at the mess hall. The outside lights were on, creating a wide, welcoming space of warmth. The director, Mrs. Harris, stood outside the front door, checking off names on her clipboard. Levi stood next to her, counting us as we passed him. Another staff member showed Levi and Terry which section of the gym-sized room was ours.

All the tables had been pushed against the wall except for one row that stood end to end through the center of the room. Two counselors were covering these tables with blankets, making a kind of privacy barrier between the boys and the girls. On top of the divider tables were two large signs: GIRLS ONLY with an arrow pointing left, and BOYS ONLY with an arrow pointing right. On both sides, chalk lines divided the Warriors' space from the Trackers.

Austin was already there, rolling out his sleeping bag. He did not look happy. If there was anything Austin hated worse than camping, it was sleeping on a hard floor. If he'd had time, he probably would have ordered an air mattress to put under his sleeping bag. Maybe a drone would deliver one to the camp any minute, straight to Austin Brockway from Amazon.

I waved to him, and he looked up and smiled. He was wearing a long-sleeved shirt with his pajama bottoms. If we could find a minute to talk, I'd tell him about the packages Jake had smuggled in. Maybe Austin would have some ideas about what was in them.

Mrs. Harris held up her hands, saying "Quiet, please. Quiet, please, campers."

Eighty campers can make a lot of noise. The blanket-covered table barrier was only waist high, so I could still see what was happening on the other side. Girls in short pajamas tippy-toed around, giggling, squealing, complaining, and whining as they tried to get settled in their allotted space. On the boys' side there were other kinds of noises: snorting, coughing, rolling, farting, laughing, and shoving each other's sleeping bags across the tile floor. Three Tracker boys crawled under the divider table and tried to peek at the Tracker girls, making them shriek.

Mrs. Harris blew her whistle. "Quiet down! Right now! In thirty seconds I'm going to start taking away swim privileges. Counselors, get ready to take down names of anyone in your section who is still talking." The noise dimmed and faded away.

"Campers, please do not go outside to the restrooms during the night. Use the ones in each corner of this room." She pointed to them, using two fingers like a flight attendant.

A girl in Warrior section A raised her hand. "Mrs. Harris, they won't shoot the cougar, will they?"

"I don't know," said Mrs. Harris. "If it keeps coming back here they might not have a choice. We can't have a mountain lion on our campground. It could attack someone. The local farmers don't want it around either. Mountain lions will eat their cattle."

"They could catch it and take it away," said another girl. "Take it somewhere far away, where there aren't any humans."

"Yeah, they could catch it and let it go in Warriors section A. No humans there," yelled one of the boys. The rest of the boys laughed. The girls glared at them.

"Enough talking," said Mrs. Harris. "Now try to get some sleep."

The lights dimmed and then went off. I knelt down and untied the strings around my sleeping bag. My eyes felt gritty. I was tired all the way down to my bones. I stretched out on my sleeping bag, ready to doze off as the rustlings and murmurs grew quiet.

"A snake!" shrieked a girl. "There! Next to that sleeping bag!"

The peaceful calm was shattered. The lights went back on. The girls screamed and scampered, trampling kids still in their sleeping bags as they ran to the front of the room. Yelling boys bolted over, under, and around the barricade to invade the girls' section.

Mrs. Harris blew her whistle again. "Boys! Back to your sleeping bags, now! Girls, stop all that screaming!" The director walked to the middle of the room, stepping carefully around sleeping bags. Her face was flushed and her fists were clenched. "Now!" She pointed to the boys' side of the barricade.

Suddenly it was very quiet. Five or six boys walked slowly back to their sleeping bags, tiptoeing with exaggerated care.

Three of the girls' counselors and Levi went to the girls' section and began to look for the snake. One by one, they unzipped each sleeping bag and shook it out.

"Here it is," said Levi, as he lifted a flowered duffle bag. "It's a garter snake." He beckoned to me. "Brockway, you want to take this snake outside? Jim, go with him."

"I'd like to go too," said Jake.

"I don't think so," said Levi. "You and I need to talk about how that snake got in here."

"Why do you always blame me?" asked Jake.

"Because you're usually the one who did it," I muttered.

Ignoring him, Levi spoke to me. "Put the snake down outside the door and get back here immediately."

"My brother isn't going out there without me," said Austin.

Levi nodded, and Austin waited by the door.

I picked up the snake, holding it firmly with both hands so it would feel secure. Jim opened the side door and I went through it, carrying the snake carefully. The poor thing was probably totally stressed from being kidnapped and dropped in a room with forty screaming girls.

Levi stood next to the door, watching us. "Hurry up, you guys. Let the snake go and get back in here."

The smell of cat was stronger than it had been before. The cougar must be very close. I put the snake down, and it slithered away. Austin and Jim moved their flashlight beams across the ground and then up into the trees. We didn't see the cat, but that didn't mean it wasn't there. In the doorway, Levi was talking to one of the girls' counselors. He waved for us to come inside. We went in, and Levi closed the door behind us.

Jake was sitting up. When we appeared, he smiled and sank back onto his sleeping bag.

The two counselors were still talking, so the three of us went into the empty kitchen. If we kept our voices low, we could talk without being heard.

"Jake was definitely watching for us to come in. Do you think he knows we're on to him?" I asked.

Jim shrugged. "Why would he? We were both in bed with our eyes closed when he came into the cabin."

"I'm guessing those packages are in the hole in that tree." I yawned. "He'll probably try to sneak out and find them."

Jim yawned too. "Probably. I don't think I can stay awake to follow him."

"Where did the packages come from?" asked Austin.

We told him about following Jake to the road and seeing him receive two packages from someone in a dark car.

The kitchen door opened and Levi came in. "What are you guys doing out here?"

"Just talking," I said. "We didn't want to keep the others awake."

"Talking about what?" Levi stood with his hands on his hips, watching us. "What took so long outside?"

I just shook my head, trying to look innocent. "I put the snake down in the grass."

"That's all?" Levi looked from Jim to Austin.

"That's all," said Jim. "We didn't want to hang around out there."

"The cat smell is really strong," I added. "The cougar isn't very far away. I'd make sure everyone uses the bathrooms inside."

Levi nodded. "We'll remind them again in the morning. You guys better get to bed. Thanks for taking care of the snake."

Austin went back to his section, and Jim and I slid into our sleeping bags. I rolled over, trying to get comfortable on the hard, tile-covered floor. It smelled like the pine-scented cleaner my mother washed our kitchen and bathroom floors with at home. The smell made me feel homesick, not for home, but for the life I'd enjoyed before we were first changed into animals. I didn't know how good I had it back then. I didn't have to worry about sprouting eagle feathers or getting bullied by Jake Parma. I didn't have to worry about getting eaten by a cougar or having that cougar shot by the sheriff. I didn't have to worry about how to tell Megan I just wanted to be friends.

The noise began to fade. Around me, most of the guys had actually gone to sleep. I let out a long breath and closed my eyes. My ears stayed open, listening.

"Gifford," said one of the girls' counselors. "Put out the flashlight."

I sat up and looked over the barrier. Megan was sitting up, pulling something over her head. Something glowed pink at the end of it. The shell necklace. She even wore it to bed. The shell part of it was glowing like a flashlight! Austin said it glowed because I was nearby and I had once been a Komodo. Megan was at least twenty yards from me, and the necklace still knew I was there. She stuffed it under her pillow and stretched out on her sleeping bag.

One of the girls stood up and walked carefully around the sleeping bags to the area where the counselors were sleeping. A counselor sat up, and I heard the rasping sound of whispers. She stood up and walked with the camper to the girls' bathroom. Some kind of girls' emergency. I didn't even want to think about that. I snuggled back into my sleeping bag and put a pillow over my head.

I tossed and turned on the hard floor and then fell into an uneasy sleep. In my dreams, I saw the tree with the big hole on one side near the bottom. The cougar was there, her head inside the hole. The tawny tail flicked and then went still. She pulled her head out of the tree and turned. Between her teeth, held by the loose skin on the back of its neck, was a tiny cub. It was blond, with dark marks over its eyes and around its mouth. There were markings on its back, too.

I opened my eyes. The huge room was dark and quiet. Everyone seemed to be asleep. The dream had seemed so real. I could almost feel the cougar's presence, the way I felt prickling on the back of my neck when someone was watching me from behind.

I got up and crept to the door. If the cougar was near, I had to try to warn her. I would try to send her a message with my thoughts, the way I had with the wolves and the turtle. Tomorrow the sheriff would be here, and he'd bring his gun. She had to go far away.

Making as little noise as possible, I slipped outside, keeping one hand on the doorknob. What I saw took my breath away. The cougar was there.

She stood like a queen, about fifty yards from me, under the tree with the big hole. She held the back of a tiny cub's neck between her teeth, just as she had in my dream. The moonlight coated her pelt with gold. Her eyes held mine as if she was waiting for something. I tried to reach her with my thoughts.

Go. Take your babies far away. Tomorrow the sheriff will come. He'll have a gun. I pictured the sheriff with his gun in my mind, so the cougar would know who I meant and what a gun looked like. *If he sees you, he'll kill you. Go far away. Stay away from humans. Be happy.*

She stayed very still, her golden eyes still fixed on mine as though she was listening. Then, as I watched, the cougar turned and loped away. I eased back through the door, closed it quietly behind me, and then crawled into my sleeping bag.

The next time I awoke, the clock on the wall read six-thirty. The cook was in the kitchen, clattering pots and pans. The smell of coffee wafted out into the big hall. Campers weren't allowed to have coffee, but it sure smelled good.

"What's Austin doing on the girls' side?" Jim stared over the barrier. "He's sitting in the middle of a bunch of girls, talking."

"Probably taking orders for purple ponchos," I muttered.

My eyes felt sticky. I forced them open and sat up. Jake's sleeping bag was empty. He wasn't in the line that was forming in front of the corner bathrooms. Jim and I hadn't found the packages. Maybe Jake had gone after them, even though he wasn't supposed to leave the mess hall. I slid on my sneakers and hurried outside.

The cat smell was almost gone. Jake was nowhere in sight. I hoped I wouldn't find him somewhere, half eaten. I hurried to the tree with the big hole and peeked inside. The hole was empty. I'd seen the cougar leave with her baby last night, but I had to be sure I wasn't dreaming.

Squatting down, I pushed leaves and twigs around and searched the area for fresh tracks. They were easy to see. Two front tracks and two back ones, right in front of the tree. That was where the cougar had stood to pick up her cub, grasping it carefully by the neck, the way cats do. Checking the surrounding area, I found more tracks. These were far apart, as though she was running. It wasn't a dream. I had really seen the cougar standing there with her cub. I hoped she'd gotten my telepathic message about the sheriff and was now safely far away.

I brushed away some leaves in front of the tree and found some different tracks. Shoe prints. Rippled soles. Sneakers.

"Looking for something?" said a voice from behind me.

I stood up and turned around. Jake stood there with his hands on his hips, watching me.

"Just looking for cougar tracks."

"You were looking for my packages."

I raised my eyebrows. "What packages?"

He glared at me, then walked away.

Back in the mess hall, I told Levi, Terry, and Mrs. Harris about the packages and the tracks I'd seen this morning.

"You should have told us about this before," said Mrs. Harris.

"We couldn't have confiscated the packages anyway," said Levi.

"We could have made him open them in front of us," said Mrs. Harris. "Campers aren't allowed to receive packages unless they are checked by the counselor or the director. That's right in the consent form that parents have to sign. Please tell Mr. Parma I want to see him in my office."

The sheriff came, and I showed him the prints that led deep into the forest. "She was running. That's why the tracks are so far apart. I think she only came back for her cub."

The sheriff sighed. "And you know this because...?"

"It's just a guess. The tracks show that she stood there for some reason." I wasn't going to tell him about seeing the cougar and sending her a mental message. He barely believed there was really a cougar.

"Okay, young man. Back to the mess hall. We'll check out the woods and let your director know if it's clear."

When I went back inside, breakfast was out on the counter. The assigned campers were taking platters of scrambled egg and sausages to the tables. I asked Levi if I could talk to him. He gestured to the seat next to him.

"I just wondered what's going to happen to Jake." I sat down next to him. "I felt bad, snitching on him."

"Nothing's going to happen to him," said Levi. "Mrs. Harris and I took him to your cabin in the Jeep. Jake showed us the boxes. Four pairs of socks, one jacket, and a book."

"What was the book?" I asked.

"*Divergent*," said Levi.

"That was already here, Levi."

The counselor sighed, then picked up his fork. "I know. We'll take care of it."

"Luke, can I talk to you a minute?" Megan followed me back to my table.

"Sure." I stopped to wait for her. Austin, who had just rolled up his sleeping bag, joined us.

"My necklace is gone," said Megan. Her voice quivered as if she was going to cry.

"You had it on last night," I said. "I saw it glowing in the dark."

"Mrs. Harris told me to put it away. So I had to take it off. Now it's gone." She wrung her hands together.

"Did you look through your sleeping bag?" asked Austin. "Maybe it fell down inside it."

"I unzipped it and turned it inside out. I took my pillow out of the pillowcase and dumped my gear bag on the blanket. I went through everything."

"Where could it go?" asked Austin.

"Three guesses." Megan stared off toward the Warrior cabins. "And they all begin with the letter J."

"How could he?" I asked. "We'd have seen him going through your stuff, wouldn't we? There were people around all the time."

"Jake took it," said Megan. "I don't know how or when, but he took it. He wanted to look at it and I wouldn't let him. He's jealous because my grandmother sent it to me."

"You're probably right, but I'd tell your counselors it's missing," said Austin. "Tell them it's a valuable keepsake. Meanwhile, Luke and I will look for it."

Megan went back to her table. None of us were supposed to leave the mess hall until the sheriff told us it was safe. Austin and I weren't worried about the cougar. I'd watched her leave with her baby during the night. By now she should be safely back in her home territory, wherever that was. Right now we had a much bigger problem. We had to find that shell necklace.

Chapter Eleven—Terror Island

It was the day of the Fish Island campout. We loaded tents, food, and sleeping bags into various boats and crossed the half-mile distance to the island. Warrior boys were assigned to row or paddle some of the younger kids over. Since all eighty of us were going, not everyone would fit in the canoes and rowboats. The camp owned four powerboats, and the counselors ferried the rest of the campers and counselors to the island in those. It took them two trips. We dropped off the girls on the east end of the island and the boys on the west end. After about an hour, everyone was on the island.

The island was a wilderness. The brush had been cut back on the east and west ends to allow canoes and rowboats to be pulled up onto the shore. Piers stretched out from both areas, where sailboats and power boats could tie up. An area on each end of the island was cleared for camping. These had picnic tables and grills for people who didn't want to cook over campfire pits.

The only building was a large concrete bathhouse with showers and toilets. It was divided in half, with space for boys on one side and girls on the other. The counselors said the bathhouse had only been there for a few years. Before that, there were wooden outhouses. One day a girl had found a snake in the girl's outhouse and got so upset she had an asthma attack. So the camp sponsors got rid of the outhouses and built the bathhouse to replace it.

Once everyone had arrived, the counselors met with their campers to give some instructions. Levi and Terry gathered the Warrior boys together near the picnic tables on the east end. The Tracker boys and their counselors came to listen too.

"We'll pitch our tents first," said Levi. "You can sleep outside if you want, but we'll have the tents up just in case it rains. The Warriors will put up their tents in this area." He waved an arm to the left of the clearing. "The Trackers will pitch their tents around the fire pit on the other side of the clearing."

"Why do we have to put the stupid tents up?" asked Jake. "We're going to sleep outside, right?"

"It's camp policy," said Levi. "We need them in case it rains or gets cold."

"What do we do if there is a storm? With lightning?" I asked. I wasn't sure what I could control anymore, and I didn't know what effect a bad storm would have on me. If I was going to morph into a Komodo or go totally eagle, I didn't want anyone watching.

"We check the weather forecast before we leave," said Terry. "If storms are predicted, we cancel the trip—like last year."

"What if a storm comes anyway, and we're already here?" I asked. "It took three trips to get everyone to the island. It would take a long time to get everyone back to camp."

"Then we send for the rescue boats," said Terry.

"What are those?" asked Jim.

Levi explained. "Several lake residents have large speedboats. They'll come and get us and take us back to camp. If we're in a hurry, we leave the tents. We can always come back and get them."

I met Jim's eyes and shrugged; that sounded good enough to me. We pitched our tents in the clearing near the west end of the island. It was a grassy place in the middle of a stand of pine trees. There were two fire pits. The Trackers would put their tents near one fire pit. The Warriors would take the other.

The wind was blowing, so we dug the campfire pits a little deeper than usual so the wind wouldn't blow hot embers into the air. We also surrounded the fire pits with rocks. Then we gathered wood for the fire. Wood was easy to find, because the entire island was covered with trees. Fallen twigs and branches were everywhere. It hadn't rained in a while, so they were dry enough to burn well.

When it was finally time to eat supper, we were all tired and hungry. We lit the fires and roasted hotdogs. The cook had sent big bags of potato chips and cartons of beans and macaroni salad along to go with the hotdogs. We passed the food around and made sure everyone was served. Then we dug in. For a while, no one spoke except to say "yum" or "pass the mustard." I'd worked up an appetite paddling across the lake. It took three hotdogs with ketchup and mustard to fill me up.

Sitting around the campfire, we told ghost stories and sang camp songs. After a couple of hours everyone was hungry again. We put together graham crackers and chocolate bars, and toasted marshmallows to make S'mores. At ten-thirty, Levi checked our fire pits to make sure the fires were out. It was past eleven when everyone finally stretched out on their sleeping bags. We lay on our backs, gazing up at the stars. It was quiet on the island, much quieter than it was in our cabin at night. The peaceful sound of waves lapping against the shore made me feel sleepy. The only other noise came from some very loud crickets and the gulping roar of a bullfrog that hung around at the edge of the water. Overhead, the dark dome of sky sparkled with stars all the way down to the horizon. Relaxed and tired, I began to drift into sleep.

The whistling shriek of something shooting into the sky yanked me from my sleepy daze. A skyrocket exploded overhead, blasting into splinters of color that rained down on us. Everyone sat up, muttering and confused. Another rocket whizzed over our heads, spiraling crazily through the air. Tiny bits of hot paper fluttered everywhere. One landed on my arm and burned it. I brushed it away. More rockets shot into the air, howling and bursting into colors. They landed around us, pieces still burning.

Somebody was shooting off fireworks. That was just plain stupid with this wind, especially in a wooded area. It felt like we were in a war zone, under attack. Blue smoke. Red smoke. More loud popping sounds. Screaming whistles followed by crashes and explosions that seemed to be coming from every direction. The air smelled of gunpowder, and kids were coughing, finding it hard to breathe. We were all up now, pulling on our shoes and jackets and trying to figure out what was going on.

In the distance, where the girls were camped, a golden haze was spreading along the treetops. It looked like the sun was coming up, but it was eleven o'clock at night. The peaceful quiet was destroyed by terrified cries from the other end of the island. The girls were screaming, "Fire! Help! Fire!"

Where was Austin? Scanning the area, I saw the Trackers boys' section moving fast, just as we were. They were heading for the lake where our boats and canoes were moored. The air was filled with confused chatter and voices ringing with panic. The counselors' phones kept ringing. Levi and Terry were talking to the other counselors on the island. Something was very wrong.

What had happened? At first it looked like fireworks. Cherry bombs. Bottle rockets. Sizzles that shot into the air and then exploded in sparkling blasts. Now it just looked like a forest fire—flames licking into the sky, lighting up the woods so we could see blackened trees falling as they burned. It was spreading fast!

"Luke!" yelled Terry. "Take the guys in your cabin and paddle two canoes back to camp. Leave the tents and sleeping bags. Keep your flashlights and lanterns on so the rescue boats can see you. Report to the director in the mess hall as soon as you get back. She'll be waiting there to check off everyone's name as you return." He gave the same directions to one person from each cabin.

"What about the Trackers?" I yelled. I didn't want to leave my brother behind.

"Their counselors will take them, and the girls' counselors are evacuating their side of the island. Don't worry. Just get moving!"

I told the guys to pack up fast. "Three to a canoe. Put on your lifejackets and turn on your flashlights and lanterns. We have to cross together. Where's Jake?"

Bill shook his head. His face was pale in the dark night. He was biting his lip. "I don't know. He left about a half hour ago. I thought he was going to the bathroom, but he never came back."

"Come on," I yelled, heading for the beach. "I'll tell a counselor to call Terry. We can't wait for him."

Then I remembered the rowboats and canoes wouldn't hold everyone. If we put five in the rowboats, they'd be too heavy for us to row. The powerboats had to make two trips to get everyone onto the island. They'd have to do it again to get everyone off. I didn't think the fire would wait for us. There had to be another plan—a faster way to get everyone to safety. Then I remembered the speedboats owned by the people who lived on the lake. They had a rescue plan for emergencies. They would be coming to help.

The Trackers were already at the shore, piling into rowboats. Their counselors were giving the same instructions I'd given. "*Lifejackets on and tied. Flashlights on. Don't worry. We'll be fine. One counselor will row each boat; Austin Brockway will row the fourth boat.*"

When I heard that, a weight lifted off my chest. Austin was okay. We were going back together. But Megan was still on the island—still in the area where the red flames now licked the sky with fiery tongues. Surely the girls were getting off the island right now too.

The Trackers shoved off one at a time, with Austin's boat in the center. The kids huddled on the seats, suddenly looking smaller and more helpless than before. Jim and I paddled with Bill between us. The other guys took the second canoe.

"Oh no," moaned Jim. "Look at that."

I turned to look where he was pointing. It looked as though half the island was up in flames. My mind began to spin with panic! Where were the girls? Where was Megan? There were forty-two girls over there, and four counselors. Had they started out? The Warrior girls and the counselors would row and paddle, but they had the same number of boats we had and more people. Jake was still missing too. I didn't like him, but I didn't want him to get caught in the fire.

One of the Tracker rowboats was only a few feet from me. I yelled to the counselor to please call Terry and tell him I couldn't find Jake Parma. He was still on the island somewhere.

The shriek of a siren pierced the air. A speedboat was coming toward us, fast. A spinning red light on its deck lit up the darkness. Now I understood why we all had to have our flashlights on. Without them, we could easily be hit. The oncoming boat swung far out and around us, but the wake still rocked us pretty hard. Other speedboats were coming too, from different directions on the lake. How would they get the fire out? There were no roads, fire engines, or fire hydrants on that island. It was strictly wilderness—and very dry. I kept paddling, trying to keep the canoe steady against the slamming waves.

"Warriors!" yelled one of the Tracker counselors. "Pull closer to us. Hold those lanterns and flashlights high!"

Jim steered, moving us closer to the Tracker boats. I could see Austin now, and knowing he was safe took away some of the panic that gripped my heart. Austin gave me a "thumbs up" signal, never missing a beat with his oars. He had enough calm for both of us. He never failed to amaze me.

I glanced back at the island and shuddered. The fire had spread even further. It had almost reached the place where we'd been camping just minutes ago. A speedboat pulled up to the pier, where a few Warriors boys and two counselors waited. They would be okay. Safe in the powerboats, they'd beat us back to camp.

Jim and I could have paddled faster, but the Tracker counselors made us stay together. It seemed to take forever to cross the lake, and by that time the emergency evacuation plan was in full swing. At least four more speedboats headed toward the island. They'd be able to pick up the rest of the campers on each end of the island, getting them all away in one trip. They wouldn't be able to put out the fire, though. It was burning ferociously, eating everything in its path.

We pulled up next to the camp's pier and dragged the canoes and boats up onto the shore. Two of the speedboats were already there, and two others were fast approaching the pier.

"Warrior section B," I yelled. "Everyone go to the mess hall so they can count heads. Be sure your tags are on the white side."

Bill joined us as we hurried up the hill. He grabbed my arm. "I need to talk to you." The muscles of his throat moved, as though he was trying to swallow something. "I'm worried about Jake," he said at last. "And there's something else. It's about those packages."

I glared at him. "Let me guess. They didn't contain four pairs of socks, one jacket, and a book."

Bill winced as if I'd hit him. "No. They contained some...something else. I told him not to do it. He said it wouldn't hurt anything. He just wanted to scare you and Austin a little. And Megan. He wanted to scare her too. He was really mad at you three for some reason."

Bill didn't have to tell me that. I already knew what was in those packages. I'd figured it out by the time the second rocket splintered into pieces of hot, burning paper and landed in the middle of our campsite.

"Why are you telling me this, Bill? You should be talking to Mrs. Harris. She's right over there by the door." I pointed at the camp director, standing in the doorway to the mess hall with a clipboard.

I checked in with Mrs. Harris and asked if we should take the boats back to pick up more kids. She said the powerboats would handle it and to tell everyone to come inside.

An ambulance raced in to the campground, lights flashing. The paramedics got out and started down the hill with a stretcher.

"That doesn't look good," said Jim.

Austin left his Tracker group and joined us. We watched from the top of the hill as the rest of the campers returned from Fish Island. Warrior girls landed their rowboats and canoes on the shore, unloading girl campers. Two speedboats pulled up behind them at the pier, dropping off the remaining Warrior boys and two Tracker boys' counselors. Three more speedboats arrived. They idled their motors just outside the pier area, waiting for their turn to pull up and unload the rest of the girls and their counselors. Levi was with them. We went down with our flashlights to see if anyone needed help.

"Don't forget to turn your tags," I yelled, as campers paraded up the long stairway. "We have to make sure everyone is back."

The paramedics carried the stretcher down the beach to a boat that was signaling with a light. They loaded someone onto the stretcher and started back up the hill toward us. When they passed us on the stairs, we couldn't tell who it was because the girl's face was covered with an oxygen mask. She didn't have red hair, so we knew it wasn't Megan.

Jim, Austin, and I spread out, holding our lanterns up high to light to the way for the girls who were coming up. Two counselors were helping another camper climb the stairs. She was coughing hard and made little squeaking sounds when she tried to breathe. Paramedics met them on the stairs with another stretcher. They helped the girl onto it and carried her the rest of the way.

Some of the kids could barely climb the long stairway. They moved slowly, coughing, shaking, and pulling on the guard rails to help themselves along. Their arms and clothes were covered with soot, and they seemed exhausted. The counselors stayed at the bottom of the stairs, checking to make sure each camper was okay. Finally all of the campers were out of the boats and on their way up the hill. The counselors followed.

Jim, Austin, and I waited on the landing until everyone had passed us. Two tags were still on the red side; one Warrior boy, and one Tracker girl.

"Did you see Megan come back yet?" asked Austin, his voice unusually tense. "I think all the boats are back and she wasn't with them."

"No. I didn't see Jake, either." I narrowed my eyes, squinting until my eyesight reached eagle vision. Scanning the water, I watched for movement. There was no sign of another boat. No movement in the water either. On the island the fire was still burning, flames licking the sky.

"I'm going over," I said. "They're on that island somewhere. They might need help."

Chapter Twelve—Rescue

"One of the counselors should go," said Jim. "I'll go get one of them."

I clamped my hand on his arm. "Don't. They won't understand. Get a boat and be ready to pick us up in a few minutes. We'll meet you out in the lake. Don't come near the shore. You might get hit with burning embers."

New feathers pricked the underside of my arms. I could feel them growing. They were long, soft feathers that would help me rise with the updraft. My heartbeat quickened, thudding against my ribcage. Everything in my being wanted to fly—wanted to get to the island as soon as I could. I closed my eyes and let it happen. Feathers rippled along my back and chest. I kicked off my shoes and gripped the ground with talons.

A surge of air flowed beneath me, lifting me off the pier. I stretched my wings out and felt the flow of air pushing me upwards. I was soaring, circling the pier. Austin waved and gave me a "thumbs up" gesture.

Below me, Austin was grabbing life jackets. Jim backed a powerboat out into the water. I had no idea who owned the boat. We were going to be in big trouble, but we had to save Megan and Jake. There was no time to waste asking permission and explaining. Especially explaining.

Flying at seventy miles an hour, I reached the island in under a minute. I barely had time to get up into the air and then down again. Huge gray clouds of smoke filled my eyes and nostrils so it was hard to breathe. I dove closer to the ground and found fresher air, but there was no sign of Megan or Jake.

They would try to get away from the fire, to get somewhere safe. The farthest part of the western section of the island—where the boys had camped—was still untouched. Rivers of flame crept closer, but I could still see open space. I flew low, scanning the unburnt area. No sign of Megan or Jake anywhere. Letting the heat collect under my wings, I rose higher into the air and headed toward the edge of the flames where the concrete bathhouse stood.

One side of the bathhouse was charred. Fire hadn't reached the other side.

"Megan! Jake!" I called their names as loudly as I could. No one answered. Maybe they couldn't hear me over the crackling roar of the fire. Or maybe they weren't in the bathhouse.

"Megan! Are you there?"

"Help!" called a weak voice. "Over here! Help!"

Swooping downward, I circled the area around the bathhouse. "Megan!" I shouted again. "Jake!"

"Here!" It was Megan's voice. "Is that Luke? Where are you?"

"Yes, it's me," I yelled. "Look outside."

"I can't see through the smoke," called Megan.

"I'm in eagle form," I said. "Get down on the ground and crawl. Follow my voice. I'll lead you to safety."

I watched the ground near the bathhouse. The smoke was getting thicker. If we didn't get out of here soon, none of us would survive.

Megan crawled out of the bathhouse and looked up into the air. She saw me and waved.

"It's Jake," she cried, looking back. "He's in the bathhouse and I can't get him to come out!"

Flying lower, I saw him. Jake stood like a statue in the door of the bathhouse, staring straight ahead. Why wasn't he moving?

"Jake," I called. "Let's go."

"It's my fault," said Jake. He spoke like a robot, with no expression in his voice. "I didn't mean to do this. I might go to prison. I might have killed someone."

"No one's dead so far," I yelled. "But if we don't get moving, we'll all die."

Megan grabbed Jake's hand and pulled him. "Let's go. I'm not turning into a pile of ash because of you!"

She turned to me in desperation. "I saw him running from the woods near the girls' side *toward* the fire. I followed him into the bathhouse, but I can't get him to morph."

Jake stared into the smoke. The fire was getting closer and closer, but he still didn't move. It was time for me to take over.

Two downward swoops brought me a couple of yards above Jake's head. I landed on his shoulders and gripped with my talons. If I could just budge him a little, maybe he'd start moving on his own. Holding tight, I flapped my wings and pulled as hard as I could. It was like pulling a six-foot bag of rocks. Wings flapping, talons gripping, towing with all my might, I managed to drag Jake about twelve inches.

Then the miracle happened. I began to rise slowly into the air. Jake's feet hung just a few inches from the ground, but at least we were moving. Megan stayed with me, hopping around the streams of fire that were invading the last part of the island as we headed toward the water. I glanced at our campsite. There was nothing left but little piles of burnt fabric where there used to be sleeping bags and a tent.

The smoke grew thicker. I dipped lower, trying to find fresh air. Jake hung limply from my talons as if he had gone into a coma.

Then I smelled something different. It smelled like burning feathers. Burning feathers? Shrieking, I dove to the sand, dropping Jake as I landed. "Megan, throw sand on me. Hurry! My tail feathers are burning!"

Megan scooped sand with her hands and tossed it on me until the fire was out. I rose into the air again, dragging Jake with me. The air grew clearer. A few seconds later we saw the water lapping up against the shore. I flew out a few feet and dropped Jake into it. He stood up, gasping and wiping water from his face.

"You'll have to swim to the boat," I called. Jake stayed where he was, dripping water.

"He won't move," cried Megan. "You won't be able to carry him across the lake. If you drop him out there, he could drown. I'll have to change forms."

She waded into the water. When she was about chest deep, she dove in. A few seconds later a beach-ball-sized turtle head broke through the water and stretched its neck to look back at the shore. A shell as big as a dining room table surfaced in the moonlit water, propelled by giant legs and claws. "Get aboard, Jake," the turtle growled. "Do it!"

"Get moving, Jake," I yelled.

Jake climbed onto the shell and sat there quietly. His face and hands were black with soot; only the whites of his eyes showed up in the darkness. He stared straight ahead, his eyes glazed in the light of the fire. He didn't speak.

The lake was calm, reflecting the orange and red flames that blazed on the island. A kind of peace surrounded us. The turtle slid through the water, making lapping sounds as the waves hit her shell. I flew ahead, leading the way toward the powerboat. I could see it several yards ahead, coming slowly toward us.

Jim slowed the boat and turned the engine down to idle. When the turtle's shell touched the boat, Austin reached over and pulled Jake across. Jake clambered awkwardly to the rear of the boat and sat down. His face was black on one side. The other side reflected the orange firelight from the island.

The turtle's head sank. Water washed over the huge shell and the turtle disappeared beneath the waves.

"I'll get Megan," I said, as my talons touched down on the boat.

"No, you won't," said Austin. "You aren't a certified lifeguard. I don't want to have to rescue both of you. I'll go."

Austin lowered himself into the water, then dove in the direction the turtle had gone. He came up several seconds later, towing Megan in a firm side grip. She was struggling against him, and she coughed and sputtered as we hauled her into the boat.

Jim patted her on the back. "If you're going to do this turtle thing very often, you should probably learn how to swim."

"I learned how to swim," Megan snapped, shaking water off her hair like a wet dog. "That's why I was trying to get away. Austin didn't give me a chance."

Jim turned the boat so we were headed back toward camp. The wind blew into our faces, drying us off as we sped over the waves. Megan huddled in the stern, next to Jake. She was shivering. When she looked at me, her eyes widened. Her mouth opened as if she was going to speak, but she didn't say anything.

I leaned my head toward Austin and whispered, "Why is she looking at me like that?"

"Dude," Austin said in a low voice. "You still have a lot of feathers. Focus and see if you can get rid of them.

I closed my eyes again and pictured myself as a human. Red hair. A little taller than last year. Nothing spectacular. I was just an ordinary kid. Except for the feathers.

I turned to Austin. "How do I look?"

Austin licked his lips. "Try a little harder."

I closed my eyes and tried again. After several seconds, I checked my hands. The feathers were gone. My feet looked like human feet, too, but I could still see feathers on my ankles. Maybe by the time we got to shore I'd be rid of most of them.

In the powerboat, it only took us a couple of minutes to get back to camp. Jim let the boat drift to the pier, then turned off the motor. Austin hopped out and tied the mooring rope to a metal cleat on the side of the pier. Megan stepped out onto the pier, but Jake sat still. He looked straight ahead, as though he hadn't noticed we had stopped.

"You can't stay there all night, Jake. Let's go." I pulled on his arm, and he stood up. He climbed out of the boat and started slowly up the long stairway that led up the hill. I followed him, pausing on the landing to turn all of our tags to white.

"Luke," whispered Austin. "Put this over your head." He handed me an old towel he'd found in the storage section of the boat.

"Why?"

"You still have some feathers that show."

"Great." I draped the towel over my head like a hood.

A sheriff's cruiser and a State Police car were parked at the top of the hill. Bill was talking to Mrs. Harris. A couple of uniformed officers stood by. When Jake appeared at the top of the stairs, the sheriff walked over and took his arm. Jake went with him quietly, still staring at the ground.

"Come on, before they see us," said Austin. "Let's hope there's no one in the bathhouse."

Luckily, the boys' bathhouse was empty. I took the towel off my head. When I looked in the mirror, I gasped with horror. Feathers covered the top of my head and the sides of my face. I couldn't see my ears. It looked like I was wearing a feather helmet. My head had gone totally eagle. I had feathers on my arms down to my wrists. Feathers covered my legs to my ankles. Was I ten percent human and ninety percent eagle now? I stared at myself in the mirror until Austin took my arm.

"Stay in the toilet stall," he said. "I'll run to my cabin and get you a hoodie."

149

"You don't have a hoodie that will fit me." I could barely get the words out. Nothing was going to cover my eagle head. It had finally happened. I was officially a freak.

It was my own fault, though. I'd used all my eagle traits to rescue Megan and Jake. If I'd taken a boat over there and tried to help them as a human, the feathers wouldn't have grown like this. But I needed the speed and the eagle vision to rescue them in time. Looking like an eagle was the price I had to pay.

Hiding in the toilet stall, I tried to think. How was I going to go home like this? Would Mom faint when she saw me? No, probably not. But she'd be very surprised. So would my dad. Maybe they'd take me to some big medical center for therapy. That wouldn't work, though. There was no medicine or treatment that would get rid of these feathers. There was only one way to get rid of them. Somehow we had to undo the curse that changed us into animals in the first place.

According to Gramps, the only way to do that was to replace the pink Komodo he'd shot to protect Dunn Nikowski. That meant we had to find a way to get to Komodo Island. Then we had to find one of the rare pink Komodo dragons. How would we do that? The medicine woman was probably dead by now. She wouldn't be able to help us. At least we had the shell necklace. Then I remembered something. Megan didn't have the shell necklace. Someone had taken it. We had to get it back. I had to make sure it was safely returned to Megan before Austin and I left camp.

Austin came back carrying a gray sweatshirt with a hood. It was exactly my size. The camp's logo was printed on the front.

"Thanks, Austin." I put it on, pulling the hood down to my eyebrows so my feathers were covered. "Where did you get this?"

"At the camp store. I bought it for you yesterday, as a souvenir. I didn't think you'd want a purple poncho."

"That was really nice of you. Thank you, Austin." I slung my arm around his shoulders and gave him a hug.

He smiled at me. For a few seconds he looked younger, like the boy who was trapped in the body of a bear last fall during those dreadful days at the zoo. He'd looked up to me then, and counted on me to help him. Things were different now. For the past week, I'd been the one needing help.

"We have to go home." I pointed to my feathered head. "There's no way I can keep people from seeing these feathers."

"I know. I've already made a call. I'll get my stuff and meet you by the road. When you've packed your suitcase, cut through Tracker camp and go down the hill. That way the crowd by the mess hall won't see you. I've talked to Megan. She knows we're leaving."

Jim was waiting for me at the cabin. "I've packed up your stuff." He nodded toward my suitcase.

"There's one more thing," I said. "I have to find a necklace made of beads with a shell pendant hanging from it. Jake has hidden it somewhere." I hoped he hadn't taken it with him to the island. If he had, it would be totally destroyed by now.

I went to Jake's bunk and picked up his pillow. There was nothing under it. I looked under his bunk and felt under his mattress. No necklace. Then I happened to look at the underside of the upper bunk. Something white, carefully folded, was tucked between the upper bunk's mattress and bed springs. A faint pink glow showed through the white fabric. I

151

reached between the mattress and the springs and carefully removed the white packet. The pink light began to blink when I touched it. Carefully, I unfolded the fabric. The necklace was there, safe in one piece. Breathing a sigh of relief, I showed it to Jim.

"So that's the shell necklace." He spoke softly, as if the necklace was something holy. Maybe in a way, it was.

"Will you tell Megan I have it?"

Jim nodded.

After wrapping it in one of my own shirts, I stuffed it carefully into my backpack. "I guess that's everything." I stood up to face Jim. Leaving him was going to be hard. We'd gotten to be good friends. I was going to miss him. And now I was leaving him at camp without a buddy.

"I'll keep an eye on that little redhead for you," said Jim. "I'll make sure she's okay."

"Tell her I said goodbye. You have my cell number?"

"Yup. I'll walk partway with you. I should be in the mess hall anyway. I don't want them sending out a search party for me."

We walked together toward the place where the path split. "What do you want me to tell the counselors?" asked Jim.

"Just tell them our dad picked up the two of us," I said. "Tell them he'll call Mrs. Harris in the morning."

"Will do, said Jim. "By the way, that's a great hoodie you have on." He plucked at my sleeve. "I don't remember seeing this before."

"Austin got it for me."

"He's a big spender, all right," said Jim. "Those purple ponchos are twenty bucks each. Where does he get the money?"

I took a deep breath and shook my head. "He learned how to invest online a couple of years ago. He could be worth maybe a half-million by now."

Jim laughed out loud. "You're kidding."

"I wish."

"A twelve-year-old kid worth half a million," said Jim. "I've never hear of such a thing." He stared at me, his eyebrows furrowed. "How much are *you* worth?"

I thought about my last bank deposit. "Two hundred seven dollars and fifty cents." We both laughed.

We had arrived at the split. We stopped there, looking awkwardly at each other. It was hard to say goodbye. I punched him in the arm and he punched me back. Grinning at each other, we shook hands. "Let's try to stay in touch," I said. Jim nodded, still smiling.

I picked up my suitcase and backpack and headed for the camp road, cutting behind the Tracker cabins to avoid the crowd near the mess hall.

"Wait, Luke," called a female voice. Megan came running down the path from her cabin. "I was watching for you," she said. "Austin told me you were leaving. I wanted to give you this before you left." She handed me a woven bracelet with leather ties on the ends. "I made it for you."

I turned it over in my hand. "Thanks, Megan. This was nice of you."

She stood there in the moonlight, smiling at me. The soot was gone from her face and her hair was wet. She looked kind of pretty. My mouth went dry. I cleared my throat, unsure what to say or do. She glanced at the bracelet in my hand, and then her eyes met mine. Did she expect me to put it on? Over my feathers? Besides, I didn't really like wearing bracelets, and I didn't want anyone asking me where I got it. I liked Megan a lot, and I didn't want to hurt her feelings. But I wasn't sure what it meant if I wore the bracelet, and I didn't want to give her the wrong idea. I didn't want other kids to get the wrong idea either. Especially Austin.

"It's really nice," I said. Even to me it sounded lame. I put the bracelet in my pocket and took the necklace out of my backpack. "I found this above Jake's bunk." I handed her the string of beads with the shell pendant. The shell glowed pink and blinked on and off when I touched it. As soon as Megan took the necklace from my hand, the blinking stopped.

"Oh, Luke! Thank you so much. I was afraid I'd never see it again." She threw both arms around my neck and gave me a hug. I patted her shoulders awkwardly and stepped away.

"Take good care of that necklace, Megan. We can't find a pink Komodo without it. And without the pink Komodo—"

"I know," she said, interrupting me. "If you can't find the Komodo, you could have those feathers for the rest of your life." She turned the necklace over and carefully touched the shell. Then she handed it back to me. "You'd better keep it then."

My whole body sagged with relief. "I'll keep it safe. I promise. I know how much this necklace means to you." I wrapped it carefully and replaced the necklace in my backpack. "I just remembered. I wanted to ask you something before I left."

Megan's eyes widened. "What do you want to ask me?"

"Did you put that snake in Jake's bed?"

"You mean that garter snake?"

I tried not to grin. "I thought it was you."

"He deserved it," said Megan. She took a deep breath and held out her hand. "So it's goodbye for now."

I took her hand. "I'm sure we'll see each other in town, at that ice cream place. We'll get Austin to buy us banana splits." We both laughed. I let go of her hand, then turned and trudged down the path. After a few steps, I looked back to see if she was still there. She was. We waved again and went our separate ways.

Austin had told me to meet him on the road, down the hill about a hundred yards, so no one would notice the car picking us up. He was there, standing on the roadside.

I dropped my heavy suitcase in a dark place under a tree. "Is Mom coming for us?"

"No. She and Dad will be asleep. We've got another ride. He'll be here soon."

We sat on the ground next to our suitcases. My stomach growled. It had been a long time since supper. A long, wild, terrible time.

"Want a snack?" Austin sorted through a pocket of his backpack and took out two peanut bars. He tossed one to me. Leather strings from a woven bracelet dangled from his wrist. I blinked. It looked exactly like mine. Maybe Megan's bracelet didn't mean anything except friendship after all. Of course Austin would be thrilled to wear it. He was crazy about her. He'd probably want one for each wrist. And maybe a head-band, too. A lump grew in my throat, though I didn't know why. I definitely wasn't looking for a girlfriend.

"Thanks," I said hoarsely. "Do you have anything to drink in there?"

"Shh," whispered Austin. "Someone's coming down the hill. It looks like Jake and some man." We watched, keeping well out of sight.

An older man yanked Jake by the arm, dragging him to the edge of the road near the main entrance to the camp. They stopped between us and the sheriff's cruiser at the top of the hill.

"Of all the stupid tricks you've pulled, this is the worst," yelled the man. "How do you think this looks for me, having a son who's in jail?" He grabbed Jake's side with his hand, squeezing it in what looked like a pinch.

"Ow!" cried Jake. "I'm sorry! Please, stop." His voice quivered as if he was going to cry. I remembered all those pinches he'd given me and how they hurt, but I still felt sorry for him.

"Shut up, you stupid cry-baby," the man snapped.

"Everything all right over here?" The sheriff stepped out onto the road and strode down to where Jake and his father stood. "You'll have to come with me, son. You can follow in your car, Mr. Parma."

They all walked back up the hill together, and we couldn't hear them anymore. Jake brushed his sleeve across his eyes. The pinch hurt, but his feelings probably hurt worse. The sheriff opened the cruiser door, and Jake crawled into the backseat. A deputy got in next to him. The sheriff turned the car around and headed down the hill. Austin and I stepped behind trees so they wouldn't see us as they drove by.

"Now we know where he got the pinching habit," said Austin. He shook his head. "Isn't that child abuse?"

"I think so. It's some kind of abuse, anyway." I thought about our dad and couldn't even imagine him behaving that way. Even if he was angry, he'd never do anything so mean.

"I'd report someone who did that to his dog." Austin pointed down the road. "I think this is our ride."

A shiny black sedan slid quietly to a stop in front of us. I didn't recognize the car. A man got out and opened the door for us. I didn't recognize him, either.

"Good evening, Mr. Brockway," said the driver. He took our suitcases and stowed them in the trunk.

"Hi, Mr. Johnson," said Austin. He introduced me to the driver, and we shook hands. "You made good time. Now let's get out of here before anybody sees us."

I saw her standing on a nearby hill, as if she was waiting for something. "Wait. There's somebody else who wants to say goodbye."

Austin came to my side. "Where?"

I pointed to a tree about a hundred yards away. "There."

The moon slid out from behind a cloud, and light poured over the area around the tree. Beneath the dark limbs stood the cougar, her magnificent blonde head catching the moonlight. From her teeth dangled a cub, held by the scruff on the back of its neck. The cat's gleaming eyes stared in our direction, and it seemed to be looking directly at us. Once again, I had the sense that she was telling me something. There were no words, but thoughts of thankfulness and well-wishing came into my head.

"You're welcome," I said aloud. "You have a great life, too." I blinked, and the cougar was gone.

"Did you say something, Mr. Brockway?" asked the driver.

"He talks to himself," said Austin. "Just ignore him."

We climbed into the backseat and fastened our seatbelts. Austin opened a small refrigerator that was built into the side of the limo. He handed me a bottle of water and another snack bar. As he stretched out his arm, the woven bracelet slid to his wrist.

"Thanks." I nodded toward the driver. "The driver seems to know you."

"Mom had his number taped to the phone she gave me. She's used his limo service a couple of times when I was with her."

I opened my backpack to make sure the shell necklace was safe. Beside it was a folded paper. "Shoot. I forgot about this."

"What did you forget?" asked Austin.

"I meant to have the counselors sign off on some requirements on my Camping Merit Badge list. I guess it doesn't matter. I'm never going to make Eagle Scout anyway."

Austin laughed out loud. "No, probably not. But you made Eagle—the real thing. You saved Megan and Jake, too. You deserve a medal for that, though you probably won't get one."

"I don't want one," I said, meaning it. "You would have done the same."

"What do you think will happen to Jake?" Austin sounded genuinely worried. "I didn't like him much, but I feel sorry for him."

"So do I. The worst thing is, Jake will probably grow up to be just like his dad."

"You think?"

I shrugged. "He already acts like him. Gramps always tells us that how we act now determines the kind of person we'll be."

"Oh, yeah." Austin leaned his head back and closed his eyes.

"You'll probably still be buying things for girls when you grow up," I said. "The girls will be grown up too. You'll have to buy bigger purple ponchos." And then I fell asleep.

Chapter Thirteen—Home is Where You Don't Have to Hide

Sunshine peeked in through the open slit in my bedroom curtains. It was almost ten-thirty in the morning. We hadn't arrived home until after three AM, and I was still tired. I stared at the ceiling, trying to wake up. Stretching, I examined my arms. The feathers were still there, on my arms and across my chest. I kicked off the sheets and checked my legs. Feathers all the way down to my ankles. Thankfully my hands and feet looked human.

I sat up and yawned. My room looked the same as it had when I left it almost a week ago. My bed linen smelled fresh and clean. Even though we were exhausted, Mom had us take showers before we got into our beds. The tubs were filthy from all the dirt and soot that washed off of us, but she didn't make us clean them up. We'd fallen into bed and gone right to sleep. Mom and Dad hadn't said anything about my feathers either. Austin had called them when we were almost home and warned them about my appearance.

The smell of bacon wafted up the stairs. Closing my eyes, I breathed in another delicious aroma. Blueberry muffins! I hopped out of bed and stopped short. A bird regarded me from the mirror. A bird with a human face. It shocked me all over again to see my head and neck covered with white feathers. There was a little red patch right on the top of my head, just as there had been red scales in that spot when I was a Komodo dragon. Megan had red hair too. Was there a red patch on that huge turtle's head last night? It was so dark out on the water that I couldn't have seen it even if I'd looked.

The bracelet Megan gave me lay on the dresser next to my backpack. She'd given Austin one just like it. Something twisted a space near my heart. She liked both of us. We were all friends. That was what I wanted, right? The three of us had been through some difficult times together. At the zoo, Austin had saved my life and I'd saved his. Megan had saved my life and I'd saved hers. The three of us were bonded together in something more than friendship. I picked up the bracelet and studied it closely. A tiny heart was tied to one of the threads. Austin's bracelet didn't have a heart. I decided not to wear it. Austin was my brother, and I didn't want him to see it and be hurt.

I put on the new sweatshirt and pulled up the hood. It covered most of the feathers. I stared at myself in the mirror. Why couldn't I just have acne? Or a jagged scar? Or a couple of moles? Why did I have to have feathers?

The doorbell rang. Familiar voices talked in the hall, saying good morning. All of a sudden I felt better. Gramps was here! He'd know what to do! I ran downstairs and straight into his arms for a big hug.

Mom hugged me too, and pulled the hood down. "You don't have to cover up here, Luke. This is your home." She

seemed pretty calm for someone whose son was ninety percent eagle.

We went to the kitchen. Dad and Austin were already at
the table, eating scrambled eggs and bacon. Austin looked up
at me with a grin. Dad got up and gave me a hug. Mom took fat
blueberry muffins out of the oven and arranged them on a
plate. I bit into one and smiled. Hot blueberries melted in my
mouth.

The first time Austin and I came home after being animals, human food didn't taste good to us. We'd gotten over
that. The food at camp was okay, but Mom's food was really
delicious. We ate breakfast and talked about camp—the good
things only. After a few minutes Austin and I couldn't think of
any more good things. We'd tossed Jake back and forth when
he was in the form of a wild pig. That was the most fun we'd
had the entire time, but I wasn't sure how Mom and Dad
would feel about that. I didn't want to tell them about Jake's
bullying. Austin didn't mention that he'd bought Megan a
twenty-dollar purple poncho. The kitchen grew very quiet.

"Tell us about this fire on Fish Island," said Mom. "How
did it start?"

So I explained about Jake getting two packages from a
man in a car, in the middle of the night.

"He hid the real contents. When our counselor and the
director checked the packages, all they found was a jacket,
some socks, and a book," I explained. "I'd seen him reading the
same book before he got the packages, so I knew he'd lied."

"Not too many people have socks delivered under cover
of darkness," said Dad. Everyone laughed.

Austin continued the story, describing how we'd seen
rockets shooting into the air and exploding into fireworks. I

told them how cherry bombs and smaller fireworks fell into our campfires, causing them to spit burning embers onto our sleeping bags.

"Fireworks were hitting the girls' camps, too," said Austin. "Especially Megan's camp. They might even have been aimed there. One of them started a fire in some brush, and it quickly spread to the trees. The counselors moved all the girls to the beach on their side of the island. The fire spread so fast the fire extinguishers were useless."

"You guys took boats back, didn't you?" asked Dad. "Didn't the girls have any boats?"

"We each had half the boats," I answered, "but they weren't enough." I explained the emergency plan and how the residents on the other side of the lake helped get some of the campers off the island with their powerboats.

"It took us a half hour to row or paddle over to Fish Island. I think they wanted us to be real tired." Austin laughed. "They didn't want any funny business going on."

"It didn't stop Jake," I said. "He must have had his backpack and his sleeping bag completely full of fireworks."

Gramps listened quietly as we discussed the fire. Then he said, "Luke, tell me more about this car that dropped off the packages. What did it look like?"

"Dark color. Nice, but not real new. That's all I could tell in the dark."

Gramps nodded. "Did you hear a voice? Was it a man or a woman?"

"A man."

"Young or old?" Gramps's expression was eager.

I tried to think. "Not a kid. Not real young." I met his eyes. "Why?"

"We have to consider another possibility," said Gramps.

I frowned. "What other possibility?"

Austin pulled his chair closer. "Who, Gramps?"

Gramps gazed into his coffee cup. "Dunn Nikowski."

"But he died. We *saw* him die," cried Austin. "We saw him die in the parking lot at the zoo."

"I've been thinking about that day," said Gramps. "If Dunn was really dead, I think his tin leg would have been left behind. He could have turned into an ant or something and gone down a crack in the pavement."

Austin and I gaped at each other. My mouth had gone dry. I tried to speak, but nothing came out. Dunn Nikowski still alive? It couldn't be. We'd all seen the enormous Gramps-hippo bite the monster Dunn-crocodile in half. We saw the big croc's tail pull away from its body and melt into the pavement like a deflating balloon.

"The crocodile's body was still there on the pavement, Gramps," I said hoarsely. "If he wasn't dead, wouldn't he have returned to his human form?"

"Yeah," added Austin. "How many animal changes could he have?"

"I don't know," said Gramps. "But I think we need to at least consider the possibility that he might still be alive."

I was so stunned I couldn't speak. My thoughts were as confused as puzzle pieces still rattling around in their box. If Dunn was alive, how would it affect us? Dunn hated us. He'd tortured Austin and me with a cattle prod when we were animals at the zoo. He'd put Megan on top of the water tower, still in her snake form. Somehow she fell, and I remembered that tiny red object dropping through the air. Without even thinking, I'd gone eagle and caught her. If I hadn't, she'd be dead.

What would Megan think of all this? Dunn had to be her grandfather, but she hated the idea. She thought her grandfather was dead and buried. What if he wasn't? Dunn was a dangerous man who didn't seem to care about anything or anyone. Suddenly I didn't feel safe anymore.

Mom came to the table with the coffeepot. Resting one hand on my shoulder, she poured Gramps more coffee, then gave me a comforting squeeze.

Gramps stirred cream into his coffee and continued. "Roy Gifford and I have been doing some research while you were at camp. We found out some interesting things."

He reached into his coat pocket and took out some folded papers, then spread them out in front of us. "Here is Dunn Nikowski's family tree. He's been married twice, so there are two different family lines. His first marriage was to someone you already know about—someone he met on the island."

I couldn't think of anyone Dunn would have known on Komodo Island. "There was the medicine woman," I said, "but Dunn was a young man then."

Austin grinned. "The medicine woman's daughter!"

Of course. Austin the love guru had the right answer. Maybe he should go to work for some internet dating service. Batman the Match Man dot com.

"Dunn was on that island for several months," said Gramps. "He married the medicine woman's daughter, whose name was Katerie. They had one child, named Angelina." He showed us Angelina's name on the paper.

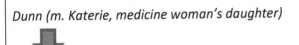

Dunn (m. Katerie, medicine woman's daughter)

Angelina

"They were very unhappy. Dunn wanted to go home to the United States, and Katerie did not want to leave the island. Eventually they divorced. Later, Dunn met and married a navy nurse named Helen." Gramps pointed to the names of Dunn's two wives and their children. Then he continued.

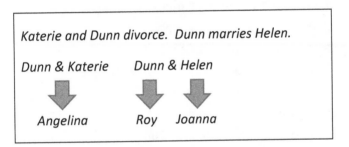

Katerie and Dunn divorce. Dunn marries Helen.

Dunn & Katerie   Dunn & Helen

Angelina   Roy   Joanna

"Dunn had two more children with Helen, Roy and Joanna. They came back to the United States with all three of the children. Later Helen divorced Dunn. She got married again, to a man named George Gifford. He adopted all three children, which is why Roy's last name is Gifford and not Nikowski. But Roy is Dunn Nikowski's son."

Gramps sipped his coffee and eyed us. "You guys got all that?"

"No," I said. We studied the rest of Gramps's diagram.

> *Helen divorces Dunn. She marries George Gifford, who adopts the three children. They take his last name. Megan's parents die. She is adopted by her Uncle Roy.*
>
> | *Angelina* | *Roy* | *Joanna* |
> |:---:|:---:|:---:|
> | *(m. Robert May)* | | *(m. Cliff Parma)* |
> | ⬇ | ⬇ | ⬇ |
> | *Megan* | *Megan* | *Jake* |

Gramps tapped the paper with his finger. "Dunn's three children—Angelina, Roy, and Joanna—were all affected by the curse. Angelina married and had a daughter, Megan, but she and her husband died soon after. Roy adopted Megan, and she took the name Gifford. Joanna married Cliff Parma, and they had one son."

"Jake!" Austin and I chimed together.

"Megan said he was her cousin," I added. "The guy's a real pig."

"That's not nice," said Mom. She hadn't met Jake.

"Maybe Dunn keeps in touch with Jake," I said. "That would explain why Jake pinched me all the time. If he thought my grandfather almost killed his grandfather, it would explain why he hated me so much."

"He pinched you all the time because his father pinched him," said Austin.

"What's this about pinching you?" Mom's voice was sharp. "Why didn't you tell us?"

"I couldn't tell anyone," I explained. "They'd have taken me to the nurse and she would have found the feathers."

"Then Jake turned that big snapper on its back and tied its legs to wooden stakes so it couldn't turn back over," said Austin. "Luckily, Luke heard...I mean, Luke found it and saved its life."

Mom bent down to hug me. "Good for you, Luke."

"There was a note on the turtle's shell, Mom," I said. "It said: *'No animal will make a fool out of me.'* When I found the note, I didn't get it. Now I remember hearing Dunn Nikowski say that."

Gramps sat back and smiled at us. "Is that how you knew Jake was related to Dunn Nikowski?"

"He had to be related to one of you," I said, "because he could change into animal form. Also, he was Megan's cousin."

"Wait a minute. Wait a minute." Austin frowned at the family tree Gramps had drawn, tracing a line with his finger from Katerie to Megan. "So this means the medicine woman's daughter is Megan's grandmother!"

I stared at the paper, watching Austin's finger tap on Megan's name.

"That was why Megan had the shell necklace," said Austin. "Dunn must have given it to Katerie. Then, many years later, Katerie sent it to her granddaughter."

I couldn't wait to show the diagram to Megan. She would be glad to see that she had some relations. Well, maybe she wouldn't be glad about Dunn. But she had a grandmother who cared enough about her to send her the necklace.

"Enough ancestry," said Mom. "We need to clear the table and load the dishwasher. You guys need to bring down your dirty laundry. Then there are two filthy bathrooms to scour."

"We'll meet this evening to make plans," said Gramps. He ran a hand over the feathers on my head. "By now I'm sure you realize what we have to do, Luke."

I nodded. "We have to go to Komodo Island to find another pink Komodo."

"We've known that for a while," said Austin. "We took a roping clinic..."

"We'll tell them about that later," I said. I didn't want Mom to know what we were planning. There was no point in worrying her with something that might not even happen.

"Komodo Island is on the other side of the world, isn't it?" I asked.

"Right," said Gramps. We picked up our plates, and he followed us to the kitchen. "Komodo Island is far away. On the way there, we'll figure out a way to find that rare Komodo dragon."

"Gramps, we have something that will help!" I ran upstairs and got the shell necklace. I told Gramps to close his eyes, then placed the necklace on the table and backed away. When the pink glow faded, I told Gramps to open his eyes.

Gramps's eyes widened and his mouth fell open. After a few seconds, he gently touched the shell.

"It couldn't be the same one," he muttered.

"What do you mean?" asked Mom.

"When Dunn was in the hospital, the medicine woman put a necklace like this around his neck," said Gramps. "It was a long time ago."

"It is the same one. Look." I took the necklace from his hands. Pink light glowed through the shell, and then it began to blink.

"We've figured it out," said Austin. "The shell glows like that when Luke is nearby. When he touches it, it begins to blink. It's because Luke has been a Komodo dragon. The necklace will help us find the pink Komodo. I'm sure of it."

"Luke will never make it past airport security," said my mother. "I'm not sure we can get him on a ship either."

"We'll get on a ship," said Gramps. "I have connections."

"So do I," said Austin. Mom rolled her eyes.

Gramps laughed. "Oh, there's one other thing. Roy and Megan Gifford will be going with us to Komodo Island. And one other person."

"Jake Parma? He can't, Gramps," I said. "He's in jail."

Gramps shook his head. "His dad is a lawyer. Jake is probably out of jail already."

"What about Dunn?" asked Mom. "Will he go too?"

"He's not invited," said Gramps. "But if he morphed into an insect or a small animal, there are a lot of places on a ship that he could hide." He put his arms around me and Austin. "Don't worry, boys. Dunn won't be allowed to bring a gun on board. And this time there will be three adults to keep an eye on him."

"You and Mr. Gifford," said Austin. "Who's the third adult?"

"Me." My mother grinned at us. "Your dad won't be coming. He has to work. Now get upstairs and clean those bathrooms."

I gaped at her. Why hadn't I realized it before? Gramps was Mom's dad. She must be affected by the curse too. Had she ever changed into an animal? I started to ask, but she just pointed to the stairs and said, "Laundry."

I stopped on the stairs and looked back at Gramps. "I know this is going to sound crazy, but I'll miss some of my animal traits."

Gramps stopped clearing the table and turned to face me. "What will you miss?"

I thought back to the previous fall, when I'd first come home from the zoo. Like the Komodo, I could smell things that were far away. "The Komodo's sense of smell helped me save that man when his boiler exploded, remember?"

Gramps nodded. "That's true, but a real Komodo would never have gone into that house. Most animals are afraid of fire. Your human courage saved that man, Luke, not the Komodo."

"Austin's grizzly bear strength helped too," I added. "While we were at camp, he saved me when four guys in my cabin all tackled me at once."

Austin shook his head, trying to tell me not to talk about that. It was too late. Mom had already heard. "What's this about four guys tackling you?" she asked.

"Football game," Austin said quickly.

"Luke, when Megan fell from the tower," Gramps said, "you changed into an eagle to catch her, even though you knew you might have to stay that way forever. Your instinctive courage made you do that."

He pointed to my brother. "And you too, Austin. Camp isn't your favorite vacation, but you went anyway, to be there in case Luke needed you. The grizzly bear didn't make that decision. It was your kind and generous human heart."

"He's very generous," I said. "He bought me this hoodie." He'd bought a few other things too, but I decided not to mention those.

"We know about all the purple ponchos," said Mom. "The man in the gift shop called us." She gave Austin a hug. "We'll have to talk about how you are using your money. Not now, though. We've had enough talking. Let's get those bathrooms cleaned."

Purple ponchos? Plural? How many had he bought? I wondered. And did that mean he wasn't as stuck on Megan as I thought? Somehow the thought made me smile.

I followed Austin up the stairs. Even being ninety percent eagle wouldn't get me excused from doing my chores. I didn't mind. The heavy feeling was gone from my chest and I felt happy again. Austin and I were back with the family who loved us. I could sleep in my comfortable bed and have blueberry muffins for breakfast. We still had a month of summer vacation left. Soon we'd be taking an exciting trip together. Gramps would help us find a pink Komodo. We'd return it to the people of Komodo Island, and that would undo the curse. I wouldn't have to look like this forever. Life was still good, even for a boy with feathers.

The End

About The Author

M.C. (Peg) Berkhousen wrote her first poem in sixth grade and has been writing all her life. She was raised in Three Rivers, Michigan, where she frequently visited the library and checked out Cherry Ames and Sue Barton nursing stories.

After graduation from Borgess School of Nursing in Kalamazoo, Michigan, Peg continued to write about her nursing experiences. She won Michigan Nurse Writer of the Year for her article on using journalism therapy with a psychiatric patient who was aboard the USS Hornet when it was sunk by the Japanese during WWII.

While working in Staff Development at St. Joseph Mercy Hospital, Pontiac, Michigan, she wrote, produced and directed staff training videos that were published by J.B. Lippincott, New York. She wrote the script and was Associate Producer for "Lincoln...In His Own Words," a project for Lincoln Life Insurance Company, narrated by actor Hal Holbrook. On faculty for Trinity International Health Services, Peg provided management training and consultation to Franciscan Sisters at Matre Dei Hospital, Bulawayo, Zimbabwe. She ended her nursing career as Director of Clinical Services, Trinity Home Health Services, and is now writing full time.

90% Human, targeted to children in grades 6th through 8th, is her second published novel and the second book of the Komodo trilogy. The first book of the trilogy, *Curse of the Komodo*, was released by Progressive Rising Phoenix Press in 2017. The third book, *Return to Komodo Island*, is planned for publication in early 2019. Peg resides in Ottawa Hills, Ohio.